Sincerely, Thatcher Hayes

JILL BRASHEAR

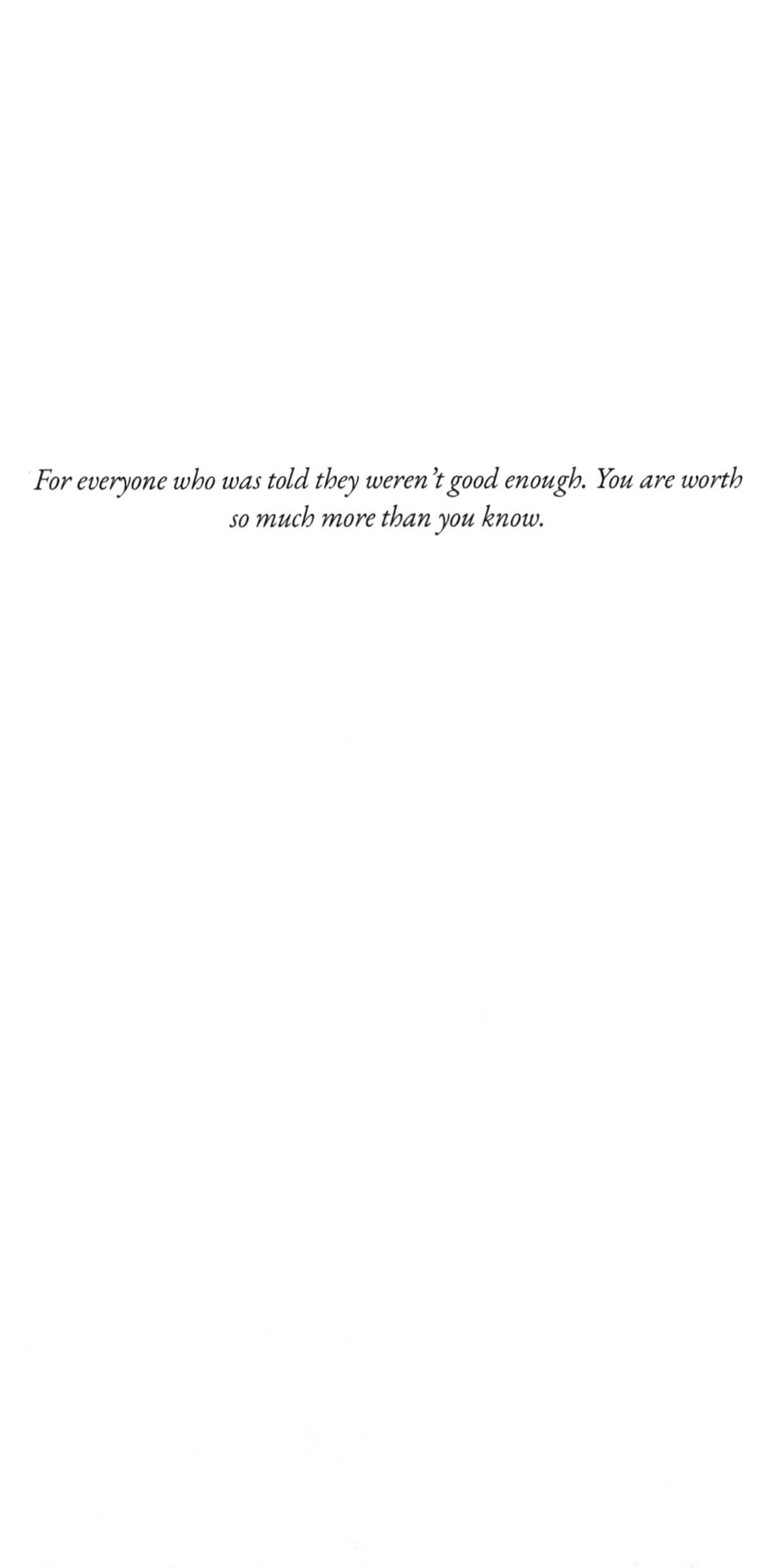

*For everyone who was told they weren't good enough. You are worth
so much more than you know.*

Preface

Hello dear readers! If you have not read Blue Collar Crush, please consider reading it first. It was written as a Prequel to Sincerely, Thatcher Hayes, and meant to be enjoyed before reading this book.

Happy Reading, Jill

One

Stripping down to my skivvies for the Men of Mossy Oak calendar may have been embarrassing, but it turned out to be a very savvy business move. That one sultry shot of me lounging on a bed of books in my boxer briefs became the talk of the town, drawing curious customers to my bookstore in droves. More often than not, they left with armfuls of books.

I'd inherited Hyperbole's Bookshop from my uncle along with the rest of his estate four years ago, and it was finally turning a profit. I liked to think my hard work in revamping the dusty old bookstore into a dream come true for book lovers was responsible for Hyperbole's success, but posing as Mr. February didn't hurt things.

Since I'd hired Lacey as manager, I spent less time in the store, but I still put in a few hours every day checking on things and working on the elaborate book displays I created.

It was a sunny Saturday morning in March with the promise of spring in the air, and the bookstore was already crowded, even though we'd just opened the doors. Customers wandered along the aisles and lounged in comfy nooks. The noise of chatter and laughter drifted along the aisles, and the scent of freshly brewed coffee and vanilla candles made the large space feel cozy and inviting.

I stopped in front of my latest window display—a tiny replica of downtown Mossy Oak, complete with the backdrop of snow-topped mountains.

"Are those clouds crooked?" I asked Lacey as she came bustling toward me with a stack of books in her arms.

She stopped and peered up at the puffy silver clouds, her eyebrows drawing together. "Definitely."

"Shit." I started toward my office, intent on grabbing my ladder and tool belt.

"Just kidding." Lacey shuffled her books to grab my arm. "It looks great."

I narrowed my eyes at the clouds. "Are you sure?" I could never stop messing with the displays. I wanted them to be perfect.

"I promise."

An elderly woman with a halo of white hair approached me with a Men of Mossy Oak Calendar in hand. I quickly signed it, trying not to cringe at the sight of myself in such a revealing state.

"What do you think, Mrs. Hellman?" Lacey asked. "Do you like the new display?"

"I love it." Mrs. Hellman shoved the calendar into her giant purse and ambled off.

"She was definitely checking out your butt," Lacey said, suppressing a laugh.

"Shut up."

"Stop being so grumpy." She shoved some of the books she carried into my free hands.

"I'm not grumpy."

"Have you been sleeping?"

"Lacey." My tone was enough to make her be quiet. "I'm fine."

She quirked an eyebrow at me, then laughed. "Your six-pack is fine. I'll give you that. And it brings in hordes of female customers. Even if they are all over sixty."

We came to the end of the local author section and shuffled through the crowd of customers on the romance aisle. "Where are you headed?" I asked.

"Historical romance."

"Ah. My favorite."

Lacey beamed at me. It was true. I was a man who loved reading romance. Especially historical. It was my guilty pleasure that was not really a secret, considering I wrote reviews for the Blue Ridge Book Club and published them online.

We got to the end of the aisle, and I stopped short, my feet rooting to the carpet.

My chest felt tight, and my skin tingled with awareness.

There she was—the woman who'd gotten away so long ago, not ten feet away from me.

She'd been beautiful when we'd first met as teenagers, but she was drop-dead gorgeous now. Her long, honey-colored hair was scooped up into an elegant bun on top of her head, with a few wavy tendrils escaping to frame her face and curl around her neck.

I'd once been lucky enough to kiss her there, where her neck met her shoulder. With a jolt, I remembered her taste.

Peppy Vinroot was fresh summer strawberries dunked in vanilla cream.

Memories of us burst in my mind like fireworks. Her lips had tasted of her dad's expensive champagne. She'd invited me into the world of her elite crowd, welcoming me with the bold assurance of a girl who got what she wanted.

No one told Peppy "no." Not her parents. Not her teachers. Especially not a scholarship kid like me in town for the summer and completely out of her league.

I'd gone willingly into her life for the short time we'd known each other. Then our time was over.

But, I'd never forgotten the summer we'd spent falling in love. So carefree and young with the world at our feet.

More than fifteen years had gone by. Peppy had been married, become a mother, and gotten a divorce.

I'd been a soldier and never married.

Since Peppy had moved back to town, every time I saw her, I felt like the wind had been knocked out of me.

"Now's your chance to talk to her," Lacey said, nudging my elbow and jostling my stack of books.

I couldn't drag my gaze from Peppy, who was bending down to examine a shelf near the floor. "I have talked to her."

Lacey nudged me again, harder this time. "Try again. I'm tired of you guys avoiding each other. It's so annoying."

I breathed deeply, fighting to regain control of the emotions running wild inside me. Every time I saw Peppy, I froze. My tongue tied, and I felt like an eighteen-year-old kid who was completely out of his league again. And Peppy went out of her way to avoid me, too. She'd once knocked over a pyramid of canned corn at Blanchard's Market, trying to steer her cart away from me.

"It's none of your business," I told Lacey.

"You need to stop tiptoeing around each other." Lacey gave me a shove in Peppy's direction. "It's giving off a bad vibe."

She was right. This was ridiculous. I was a grown man. I'd been to war and faced down rebels with machetes; I could talk to my former summer fling. Even if I had stood her up after taking her virginity. That was ages ago.

I took a determined step in her direction.

She looked up, our eyes met, and I felt like I'd been struck by lightning.

Her eyes saw straight through me, shining a light on all the faults I'd shoved to the shadows.

My failures.

My mistakes.

My fears and anxieties.

Jesus. The letters. I'd almost forgotten about the letters I'd sent to her from Africa. I'd spilled my soul to Peppy in those sappy letters. I couldn't remember exactly what I'd written, but god knows it was embarrassing.

Panic seized me, cutting off my air supply. Had I written about the reform school disaster? The answer hit me like a punch to the gut—yes.

Yes, I had.

Two

A giddy thrill ran down my spine at the sight of Thatcher Hayes. He was the physical embodiment of my fantasy man. His hair was long, falling in rich golden waves nearly to his shoulders. Trim and fit, he had the lean body of an athlete, not a meathead made in the gym.

And that face. That gorgeous face with its stupidly symmetrical features and annoyingly square jaw. He was too perfect. Too pretty.

He made my mouth water, my knees weak, and my panties wet.

Shit, he was coming toward me, chatting with Lacey Donovan over the mountain of books he carried. Was there anywhere decent to hide?

I couldn't talk to him. I wasn't that girl he'd known who'd strutted around town like she'd owned the place. Back then, I'd been a ten with daddy issues. Now, I was maybe a six with enough baggage to fill a moving truck.

Our eyes locked, and emotions crackled between us. I froze. He froze. But the woman behind him kept going, bumping into him and causing him to drop his stack of books.

It was the perfect moment for me to escape.

I practically ran out of the bookstore, knocking people out of my way like a pinball on a mission. What had I been thinking coming into the bookstore? It was the one place in town I was almost guaranteed to have a Thatcher Hayes sighting.

Flinging myself into the safety of my car, I ignored that nasty voice in my head that insisted I'd gone to the bookstore with more than the intent to buy a book for my daughter, who was currently not speaking to me. That voice said I wanted to see Thatcher, and dammit, that voice was too smart for her own good.

Thatcher Hayes had been my first crush. My first lover. My first heartbreaking disappointment.

There'd been other heartbreaks since him. Most notably, my ex-husband, Jeff, who'd thought it was okay for a married man to have a Tinder profile.

I was a coward for avoiding Thatcher, but I did it out of survival. A conversation with him might have killed me.

That voice said I was being a drama queen, but that voice hadn't been around when Thatcher had stood me up and never spoken to me again after I'd given him my virginity.

My heart broke again for that girl I'd been. She'd gone home to an empty house after waiting for hours for Thatcher to show up. She'd drunk too much wine and cried herself to sleep, only to wake up with a raging hangover and a broken heart.

Almost two decades had passed, and I still remembered how miserable I'd been. I could handle heartbreak much better now.

After being married to Jeff, I'd become an expert.

Starting up my car, I drove away from Main Street. I didn't have to be at work for a few more hours, but I may as well go in early. I had nothing else to do.

Summer was at school—probably still pouting about the fight we'd had that morning. She'd wanted to quit ballet, and I had flat out refused.

"Quitting isn't an option," I'd said.

"You quit being married to Dad," Summer had said.

Hours later, her comment still stung, but I hadn't changed

my mind about ballet. Summer needed structure in her life to make up for the messy divorce and our recent move to Mossy Oak. Ballet provided that structure. It was good exercise, and it was social. For a couple of hours a few times a week, I knew Summer was moving her body and interacting with other kids instead of curling up in a corner with her nose buried in a book.

With some time on my hands to kill, I indulged in my favorite pastime since moving back to Mossy Oak. I stalked my favorite neighborhood for a house to buy. One of these days, a For Sale sign was going to pop up on one of the long, grassy yards.

Summer and I, along with our rescue pup Aslan, were staying with my brother until we found a place of our own. Although Beckett's ten-thousand-square-foot mansion in the hills of Sapphire Valley had plenty of room for us, it wasn't ideal.

The location was inconvenient, there was no fenced-in yard for Aslan, and Beckett had no qualms about interjecting himself into my personal life. For a man who'd just gotten his first serious girlfriend, my younger brother was very full of relationship advice.

It was past time Summer, Aslan, and I found our own space. Preferably in the charming, historic neighborhood of Dogwood Hills.

Although Main Street was livelier than it had ever been, Mossy Oak was still the sleepy town I remembered. Coming home had been the warm hug I'd needed.

Mossy Oak had grown since I'd left, but it still had that small-town feel I loved so much. People knew each other in Mossy Oak. They looked out for their neighbors. There was a sense of belonging here that I'd never experienced anywhere else.

Add the small-town goodness to the perfect location in the scenic Blue Ridge Mountains, and Mossy Oak was the ideal place to raise a family.

Too bad I didn't have the perfect family to go with the town. I'd envisioned myself with a handsome husband, a fulfilling career, and a house full of well-adjusted children.

I had the career; but was sadly lacking in the husband and kids departments.

My chest tightened as I turned onto my favorite street in the neighborhood. Sweet Gum Lane was the most beautiful street in town. The homes were a mix of charming bungalows and traditional brick Colonials. Large oaks shaded the wide streets where children played street hockey. Neighbors chatted over neatly kept hedges, and tire swings hung from the sturdy branches of sugar maple trees.

I rolled down the window and breathed in the smells of spring. A slight chill dampened the air, but the dogwoods were blooming, and tulips burst from window boxes.

I'd been conditioned to drive slowly on the street by a grumpy old man who'd sat on his porch yelling at everyone to slow down. The old man, who'd been ancient twenty years ago, was probably long gone. But my dream house was still right next door, looking just as charming as I remembered.

The white wood and black shutters had been freshly painted, and the wide front porch was just as inviting. I could imagine myself in one of the rocking chairs, sipping a glass of Southern sweet tea.

My heart jumped to my throat, and I slammed on the brakes. In the sprawling front yard of my dream house was the sign I'd been waiting for.

"For Sale."

Three

The smell of the place hit me immediately. Jay kept the gym so clean; it always smelled of Pine-Sol and bleach, no matter how much blood and sweat had been spilled on the mats.

I said hello to Tracey, the receptionist who was the only one who could talk shit to Jay and get away with it, and made my way to the ring, where Manny "Killer Bee" Perez was warming up.

Manny was the best fighter to come out of the gym. His name was on a banner hanging from the ceiling, and his face was plastered on the walls. He was headlining Fight Night, but he was as humble as they came.

His head came up as I passed, and he beckoned me over. "Help me tape up?"

I dropped my duffel bag and climbed into the ring. "Where's Jay?" I asked.

"He had to take a call," he said. "But Beckett will be here any minute, and I ain't got time to waste."

As I wound the tape around his hand, securing the gauze in place, I had a flash of regret that it wasn't me training for a fight. Although I still loved the sport of boxing, I was unofficially retired. It would never be me again in the ring. Not after the beating I'd taken last time.

"You'll be ready," I said, finishing up the wrapping on his right hand before moving on to his left.

Manny nodded grimly. "I stay ready."

I didn't doubt him. Manny was lean and mean, with a tattoo of an angry bee across his throat. He was seven and zero in professional boxing, and his last four fights had been knockouts. His opponent was a heavy hitter, a guy they called the Hitman because of his deadly punches.

Fight Night was going to attract a huge crowd. Tickets were almost sold out, and it was still months away.

I finished wrapping Manny's hands and helped him with his gloves.

"You need me to stand in for a minute?" I moved toward the pads in the corner automatically, my adrenaline pumping at the thought of going a few rounds in the ring.

"Nah." Manny lifted his chin, gesturing behind me.

Beckett approached, striding purposefully across the room with a phone glued to his ear. Behind him trailed a wisp of a girl with thin arms and legs and a pixie hairstyle—his niece.

In looks, Summer Carleton was a miniature version of her mom. She had the same heart-shaped face as Peppy, the same wide-set blue eyes, and determined chin. But that was where the resemblance ended. Peppy exuded the confidence of a graceful jungle cat. Summer was a skittering squirrel.

The first time I'd met her, she'd barely been able to meet my eye. But she'd become a frequent customer at Hyperbole's, and we'd become friends. We'd bonded over our love of books and fondness for the café's hot cocoa with marshmallows on top.

Summer was the kind of kid I'd designed the young adult section of Hyperbole's with in mind. A voracious reader, she was working her way through the young adult fantasy shelves in alphabetical order.

"Hey, Winter," I said.

At the sound of her nickname, Summer's head snapped in my direction. Her blue eyes were bright with curiosity before shyness took over, and she concentrated on her shoes.

"Hi, Mr. T."

"What letter are you up to now?"

Her chin lifted, and her eyes met mine. "*P.*"

"Did you get to Paula Patterson yet?"

She nodded with enthusiasm. "I already finished all of hers."

"Hmmm. What about Stephanie Percy?" I asked, referring to a popular author of a series about mermaids in space.

Summer beamed, looking even more like her mother when she smiled. "I'm on book four."

"Read it slowly," I advised. "Because the final book might not come out for a few years."

Her smile dropped. "Oh, no."

I nodded with sympathy. "Percy is known to be a very slow writer. It took her seven years to write one book."

Horror stamped on her face. "That's almost my whole life."

"Writing books isn't easy," Beckett said, putting his hand on his niece's shoulder. "Cut Stephanie some slack."

"But I can't move on to the next letter until I read the rest of her books," she said with all the drama of a preteen girl. "I'll be stuck on *P* forever."

Beckett and I exchanged an amused glance over her head as Jay approached. "You guys gonna stand around all day?" he asked, his gruff voice startling Summer back inside her shell.

"Getting to it right now, boss man." Beckett climbed into the ring.

"Don't call me that." Jay looked down from his lofty height and seemed to notice Summer for the first time. "You here for Champion's Corner?" he asked, cocking his head at her. "Because you're late. Training started ten minutes ago."

"She's my niece," Beckett said. "Just waiting on her mom to get here."

At the mention of Summer's mother, my heart rate doubled.

Pressly was coming here, and soon. At least I had advance warning.

"What's Champion's Corner?"

Jay climbed into the ring and checked Manny's gloves. "Thatcher will show you," he said. "Take her around, will you?"

As owner of Out of the Box, Jay was always trying to recruit new members. Especially members who looked like they could afford to pay the membership fee. The paying clients allowed the scholarship kids to have a spot in the program.

"Come on," I told Summer, leading her through the crowded gym to where a group of kids were jumping rope. "You can see for yourself."

Her mouth dropped open. "You let kids train here?"

I laughed at her shocked expression. "Yeah, we do."

Summer's gaze snagged on a young girl not much older than her with a long, rainbow-colored ponytail. "You let girls in the program?"

"Sure."

"But I thought fighting was only for boys?"

"The kids don't fight. They box. And boxing is for both girls and boys."

Summer watched with fascination as the kids paired up and began going through punch combos. "What if they get hurt?"

I shook my head. "You are just as likely to get hurt in ballet as you are while training for boxing."

Summer's nose wrinkled. "I wish I would get hurt in ballet," she said. "Then maybe I wouldn't have to go anymore."

"Don't you like ballet?" I asked.

"I would rather get poked with porcupine quills."

I sat on a bench and pulled out my high-top trainers. "I guess that's a no?"

Summer sat next to me and rested her elbows on her knees. "I would rather have my eyelids super-glued open and be forced to watch a Harry Styles concert."

I snorted a laugh. "So I guess you don't like Harry Styles?"

She scoffed. "I would rather..." Summer launched into a list of things she'd rather suffer than attend a Harry Styles concert, and my mind drifted to her mother.

Peppy would be here any minute, and this time, I wasn't letting her get away without a conversation. We'd avoided each other long enough. I had to face the fact that she'd read those embarrassing letters and possibly thought I was worse than shit on the bottom of her shoe.

"Do you think I could be in Champion's Corner?" Summer asked.

I paused and scratched my chin, looking at her with a somber expression. "Are you between the ages of eight and fifteen?"

She responded with a vigorous nod that sent her hair swinging around her chin. "I'm nine."

"Perfect. Then you are welcome to join. You just have to get your mom's permission."

Summer crossed her arms over her chest and poked out her chin. "She probably won't let me. She never lets me do anything."

"She lets you buy as many books as you want," I said. "That's pretty awesome. And she got Aslan for you. You love Aslan."

Summer's face brightened at the mention of her beloved rescue dog, and she seemed to consider the idea that her mom wasn't so bad after all.

"Why don't you try asking her before you assume she'll say no?" I suggested. "Closed mouths don't get fed."

Her eyebrows disappeared under the fringe of her bangs. "What does that mean?"

I laughed and ruffled her hair. "It means ask for what you want or go hungry."

She considered me for a long moment, then hopped up from the bench. "Okay. I will."

Weaving around the people training, Summer ran across the gym to where her mother stood at the reception desk. I got to my feet, following at a much slower pace.

She was dressed for work in a professional suit and high heels. Her hair was artfully arranged on top of her head in a style that was both effortless and elegant. She stood with perfect posture, ignoring the many looks directed at her like a princess among commoners.

Peppy Vinroot, with her polished air and effortless grace, was like a beam of sunlight. Just a little too bright for my eyes and hot as fuck.

I set my jaw and strode toward her, giving myself a little pep talk with each step.

Deep breaths, you cowardly fucker.

Don't be a loser.

Own your shit.

Peppy didn't see me at first. Her gaze was trained on her daughter. A sweet smile curved her lips, and a spark of joy lit her eyes.

When she looked up and saw me, her expression transformed. A curtain fell over her eyes, and her smile frosted over.

Yeah, I was worse than shit on her shoe.

"Hey, Mom?" Summer tugged Peppy's blazer, drawing her gaze away from me. "Can I join Champion's Corner?"

"You can tell me all about that later," she said, turning Summer to the exit. "It's time for ballet."

"But I really want to do it. I'm between the ages of eight and fifteen. Mr. T said that's all it took."

Peppy's gaze snapped to mine. "Did he?"

"I want to know all about it," Summer said. "Please!"

"We'll discuss it later," Peppy said. "Come on, now. We don't want to be late."

Summer yanked her hand away from her mom's. "I'm not a baby."

Peppy's eyes met mine again, and I saw the quick flash of pain before she hid it.

I took a step forward, wishing I could close the physical and emotional distance between us. "Peppy."

She froze, then slowly lifted her chin to look down her nose at me. "No one calls me that anymore. It's Pressly now."

A chill settled in the air between us, and the distance I'd hoped to erase grew exponentially.

"I'm sorry," I said. "I forgot." We'd spoken exactly once since she'd moved back to Mossy Oak, and she'd made it clear her nickname was in her past. "When you have some free time, give me a call. I can tell you all about the kids program. I help with the training sometimes."

Pressly stared at me, her icy expression chilling me to the bones. "I don't have a lot of free time," she said.

"What's your number?" Summer asked, whipping out her phone.

I recited my number, shamelessly using a nine-year-old girl to get my foot in the door with Pressly. It was a new low for me.

But as mother and daughter left the gym, I didn't feel low. I felt hopeful.

Four

As manager of a world-class resort with a five-hundred-room hotel, exclusive spa, and five-star restaurant, I worked long hours and loved every minute of them.

Since I was a little girl, I'd dreamed of being in charge of Sky Valley Resort, which had been in our family for generations. I'd been fascinated with the grand lobby of the hotel, the sweeping hills of the vineyards, and the elegant restaurant that attracted celebrities, presidents, and princesses.

Much to the disappointment of my father, I'd studied hotel and restaurant management in college. Since then, I'd worked my butt off, sacrificing my time with my family for my career to climb to senior positions in the industry. But still, my father refused to hire me. It wasn't until my predecessor embezzled tens of thousands of dollars from the resort that I got the opportunity to manage the resort.

Thank God for Beckett because he'd convinced our dad it wasn't only the right move, it was the only move. They needed a quick replacement and to keep everything quiet. Turned out there was no one like family when it came down to it.

I'd been manager for a few months, and it was a perfect fit. I loved the resort, and it showed. The staff had been wary at first, considering it was my brother who signed their checks. But when I'd given the best office at the resort to the events manager and turned a tiny supply office in the bowels of the kitchen into my headquarters, they'd looked at me with new respect.

Slowly but surely, they were coming to respect me. My office door was always open.

There was a quick knock, followed by the widening of the door. Sloane Smith, events manager with the primo office space, stepped inside. "Do you have a minute?"

I closed my laptop and folded my hands on my desk. "Of course."

"I'm having these gift baskets done up for a yoga retreat." She strode across the room and put a basket on my desk. "Giovanni is refusing to make rice crispy treats."

I reached for the basket and pulled out a strip of candy-colored condoms. Raising a brow at Sloane, I held up the condoms. "A yoga retreat?"

"You'd be surprised." She smiled. "These yogis tend to get a bit wild."

She showed me some of the other items—a meditation journal and pen, a bottle of atmosphere mist, a jar of local honey, and a calendar.

"I thought it would be nice to have some in-house treats made. Some of the yogis are gluten-free."

Curious, I picked up the calendar. The cover featured a man in his underwear reclining on a bed, holding a kitten. The title, "Twelve Men of Mossy Oak," was printed in bold letters. My cheeks heated as I recognized him as the man from the animal shelter where we'd adopted Aslan.

"What's this?"I flipped through the calendar, pausing on the month of April, which featured a fireman wearing nothing but his tighty whities standing next to the fire truck.

"That's the calendar we do every year. You haven't seen it yet?"

I turned to September and got a glimpse of the owner of the

chocolate shop in his macaron-decorated boxers before shutting the calendar and placing it face down on my desk.

"You're gonna want to see February," she said.

Dread filled me. "It better not be my brother."

Sloane tapped her lip with a french-tipped nail. "Great idea for next year. But no, it's not Beckett."

I couldn't resist picking up the calendar and flipping to February. The rush of heat on my cheeks spread through my entire body at the sight of Thatcher reclining against a stack of books, in his boxers. His toned muscles and gleaming skin made my mouth water.

I slapped the calendar closed and tossed it back into the basket. Too late—the image was already burned on my brain. I couldn't unsee the long, lean lines of his thighs or the washboard abs.

"You can keep this," Sloane said, shoving the basket toward me.

I blinked to clear my mind of the vision of Thatcher in all his glory and folded my hands on my desk. "Leave Gio to me," I said.

Gio agreed to compromise on the food for the yoga retreat, and the rest of the day went smoothly. When the night manager arrived, instead of dropping home to change, I headed straight to pick up Summer from ballet. If I arrived early, I could catch the last thirty minutes of practice.

I drove along Main Street, trying not to think of Thatcher in his boxers when I passed Hyperbole's.

But it was impossible.

Heat blasted my cheeks, forcing me to roll down the window. The cool night air did little for my inner temperature, which rose to heat stroke level every time I thought of Thatcher in the calendar. It had been years since I'd seen him shirtless, and he'd only gotten better with age.

Damn Thatcher for being untouched by the years that had been so hard on me. It would serve him right to be bald and fat for standing me up and breaking my heart.

The pain and disappointment Thatcher had caused me as a young woman was nothing compared to the humiliation I'd suffered at the hands of my cheating husband, but even after all these years, it still hurt.

I passed the bookstore and turned onto Mountain Laurel Lane, parking in front of Miss Donna's Dance Studio.

Pushing thoughts of Thatcher to the back of my mind, I went into the studio and joined the parents in the viewing room. A dozen little girls in pink leotards and tights lined up at the barre. Their toes pointed and flexed in unison, arms rising gracefully as the instructor called out positions.

I scanned the little blonde buns for Summer's chin-length bob, but I didn't see her. She was not in the line at the front of the room, so I craned my neck to peer at the second row.

When I realized Summer was not in the second row, nor was she anywhere in the room, my blood ran cold. I shifted in my chair, searching the faces of each ballerina again.

"You're Summer's mom, right?"

I dragged my attention away from the girls and looked at the woman next to me.

"Yes," I said. "Summer must be in the bathroom?" My voice came out high and tense, the question hopeful.

"I think she left early," the woman said.

Nausea quivered in my stomach. "What?"

The woman's brows pinched together. "She left about thirty minutes ago."

I jumped up from my chair, heart beating out of my chest. "Where did she go?"

"I'm not sure." The woman's face creased with concern. "Is there a problem?"

My mind swam with panic. I took a deep breath and shoved down my fear. It was hard not to jump to the worst scenario. I pictured Summer being kidnapped or murdered, but then I reminded myself this was Mossy Oak, a safe town where people looked out for children as if they were their own.

I pulled in a deep breath, forcing air through my tight lungs. "I'm sure everything is fine," I said.

"Oh." Her face relaxed. "The girl from the bookstore with the tattoos usually drops her off. Or the tall guy with glasses?"

I was lucky to have help with Summer. Being a single mom wasn't easy. I'd hired Lacey as a dog walker when we'd adopted Aslan, but she'd become a good friend and a reliable babysitter, and Beckett deserved the brother of the year award.

"Lacey Donovan," I said. "And the tall guy is my brother, Beckett."

"He's very handsome," she said, a blush creeping up her cheeks.

Pulling out my phone, I saw a missed call from a local number I didn't recognize. "I must have gotten my days mixed up."

"I do that all the time," the woman said, her voice sympathetic. "Busy mom life, right?"

I nodded and excused myself to call the number.

"Hyperbole's Bookshop. How can I help you?"

Relief made my vision swim. "Is Lacey Donovan available?"

"Sure. Give me just a second."

I paced to the exit and pushed open the door. A cool blast of mountain air hit me as I stepped outside. The temperature had dropped as the sun set, and I hoped Summer was wearing a coat.

My scalp prickled with fear, and I forced myself to remain calm. I'd moved to Mossy Oak for a fresh start, but maybe I'd been selfish. Maybe I should have stayed in Atlanta, where my job didn't require such long hours and Summer's dad lived close by. Maybe I should have—

"Hello? This is Lacey."

My breath came out in a rush. "Lacey! It's Pressly. Summer's not at dance. Do you know where she is?"

"She showed up here a little while ago," Lacey said. "She said ballet got finished early. I thought it sounded a little fishy since Miss Donna never lets them out early, so I called you."

My heart stopped slamming in my chest, and I exhaled with relief. "She's still there?"

"Yeah. She's settled in the loft in her favorite chair."

Panic gave way to frustration as I pictured the cozy scene. "I'll be there in a minute," I said. "Keep an eye on her until I get there, okay?"

"Of course," Lacey said. "Don't worry. She's fine."

Tension crept up my neck, and the beginning of a headache pulsed behind my eyes. I opted to walk instead of drive. The brisk air and movement would help clear my head. It also gave me a chance to come up with a suitable punishment for Summer.

Because although Summer was fine for the moment, that wasn't going to last. She wouldn't be fine when she found out she was grounded.

Five

Summer and I were in a heated discussion over our favorite character in Stephanie Percy's books when she suddenly jumped up from her chair.

"Oh, my gosh!" She grabbed her backpack and slung it over her shoulder. "I have to go."

Daisy lifted her head and thumped her tail, watching Summer with her big brown eyes.

"Where's the fire?" I asked.

Summer bent and gave Daisy an absent pat on the head. "I just gotta go. My mom is picking me up."

"Lacey isn't taking you home tonight?" I'd assumed Summer was hanging out in the Young Adult section until Lacey finished working.

Summer shook her head. "See you later, Mr. T," she said, hurrying to the stairs. "And Janarena is definitely the best mermaid."

I laughed, but the sound died away as Pressly came into view at the top of the stairs. She strode toward us with perfect posture, her back straight and the long column of her neck exposed by the high tilt of her chin.

My throat was dry, and my tongue felt thick. Every time I saw

Pressly, my body betrayed me. I reverted to a teenage boy intimidated by the girl he was crushing on.

Her blue gaze landed on me for a moment, narrowed slightly, then shifted back to Summer. "What's going on here?"

Summer's shoulders tensed, and a blush crept up her cheeks. "Nothing."

Pressly's gaze dropped over her daughter's guilty expression. "Why aren't you at ballet?"

Summer shrugged. "It got out early, so I walked over here. I was about to go back and wait for you."

Pressly arched an eyebrow. "Why didn't you call me and let me know?"

Summer's eyes narrowed. "You were at work. You're always at work."

Two bright spots of color appeared on Pressly's cheeks. "You're supposed to be at ballet."

"I hate ballet. I'm horrible at it, and Maddie says I'm the worst dancer she's ever seen. Worse than a toad."

"Maddie sounds like a little shit," I muttered.

Summer's eyes widened, and she gaped at me. "You're not supposed to say that."

I shifted back a step and put my hands in my pockets. "Sorry."

A giggle escaped Summer's mouth. "It's true, though. Maddie is—"

Pressly interrupted her daughter. "Let's go," she said. "And I don't want you coming here on your own anymore. Not without an adult."

Summer's jaw clenched, and she hugged her book to her chest. "I'm not a baby. You're always treating me like a baby. Lots of kids hang out here." She turned to look at me. "Don't they, Mr. T?"

Before I could answer, Pressly silenced me with a scowl. "This isn't about the bookstore," she said.

Summer implored me with a look, but I shook my head. "Listen to your mother," I said.

"So, I'm not welcome here anymore?" Summer asked, her lower lip quivering.

"Of course you are," I said, feeling stuck between a rock and a hard place.

Pressly gave me a cool look. "Are you in the habit of allowing unsupervised children to run amuck in your bookstore, Thatcher?"

I was pathetic for how happy it made me to hear her say my name. It was like getting my foot in the door. A teasing smile curved my mouth. "The children of Mossy Oak are a wild bunch," I said. "But they don't usually cause too much damage."

Pressly spared me a blistering glance, then turned to her daughter. "Summer, go wait for me downstairs with Miss Lacey."

"Why?" asked Summer.

Pressly gave her the standard mom answer. "Because I said so."

Summer hunched her shoulders and trudged down the stairs. "Bye, Mr. T," she said.

"Bye, Winter."

When Summer was gone, Pressly turned to me. "I would appreciate your support on this," she said.

I took a step closer, feeling drawn toward her by an invisible force. "You got it."

She rubbed her forehead as if trying to ward off a headache and peered up at me. "I don't know how you did it, but somehow you've made friends with Summer. She likes you."

I smiled. "I like her, too."

She pressed her lips together, stifling a sigh. "She can't come here without an adult," she said. "Me, my brother, Lacey... someone has to watch over her. It's not safe."

"I totally get that."

Her gaze hardened. "You have no idea how I felt when I saw

she wasn't in ballet. It took years off my life. And she's up here reading like it's nothing."

I was dying to touch her, to let her know she had my support. "I understand."

She cut her eyes at me. "Not really."

I smiled. "I'm trying." I glanced down at the first floor, where Summer stood at the register. "If she ever comes in here alone again, I'll call and let you know right away."

"I'd appreciate that."

"I probably need your number," I said.

She flushed and pulled out her phone. Tapping the screen, she opened a new contact and handed me the phone. I entered my number and handed her phone back. Our fingers brushed, and she pulled in a deep breath, her chest heaving.

A spark flared down my spine, and I felt the throb of sexual chemistry draw us closer. She called my number, letting it ring once before hanging up. "There. Now you have it."

I held her gaze, and electricity sparked between us. She took a quick breath, her chest rising and falling rapidly. She was close enough for me to smell the subtle fragrance she wore. It was feminine and flirty, definitely expensive, and it made me desperate for more of her.

Pressly was the one who'd gotten away. The girl I wrote letters to from overseas that went unanswered. The one who haunted my dreams and stirred my desire even more after all these years.

"Now that we've got each other's numbers, maybe we could meet for a drink sometime," I asked. "Or dinner?"

Her gaze flicked away from mine. "Why?"

I'd never been good at lying, so I didn't bother. I needed to tell her how sorry I was for being one of the men in her life who'd hurt her, but this wasn't the time or place. "I'd like to see more of you."

Her mouth moved into a smile that didn't quite reach her eyes. "You want to start up where we left off."

My entire body tightened at the thought. Her lips on mine.

My hands on her body. Our worlds colliding and tangling together. "Would that be so bad?"

She clasped her forearms, elbows pressed tightly to her sides as if she was trying to protect herself. "There's zero chance of that happening."

Beckett had mentioned what a tough time Pressly had been through with her divorce, and I could see the pain and distrust written all over her face.

I lifted my shoulders, shrugging as if her rejection didn't gut me. "It's just a drink."

She started down the stairs. "I don't have time for drinks," she said.

For people like you. The words hung unspoken in the air between us, but I got the message loud and clear. I hadn't been good enough for Pressly the first time we'd met. And it looked like nothing had changed.

Six

Pros:

- Move out of Beckett's place
- A yard for Aslan
- Make all the decisions
- Long-term investment
- Tax benefits
- Location close to town
- Neighborhood has lots of kids
- Dream home on Sweet Gum Lane

Cons:

- Solo home owner
- Older home may need more maintenance
- I'm not handy
- Less mobility when owning
- Longer commute to work

After considerable deliberation, I called the listing agent and booked a tour of the home on Sweet Gum Lane. We had an appointment for 3:30, right after I picked Summer up from school.

"Why are you here?" she asked when it was me instead of Lacey or Beckett.

I forced a smile. "I have something to show you."

Summer greeted Aslan with a hug and kisses on his square head and floppy ears. He responded with a tongue bath that had her giggling. The sound was enough to make my heart soar and my smile genuine. Thank God I'd brought Aslan. He always helped break the ice between me and Summer.

After being grounded for a week for skipping ballet, Summer was officially free, but she still preferred to go straight to her room after dinner and was hardly speaking to me.

Worry was my middle name when it came to Summer. I worried that she didn't have any friends. I worried over her obsession with reading. Most of all, I worried that she would hate me for the rest of her life.

As soon as she was buckled in, Summer pulled her book from her backpack and started reading.

"You shouldn't read in the car," I said.

She turned the page. "Why not?"

"It's bad for your eyes."

"Lacey lets me."

I let that one go and tried another tactic. "You'll miss what's around you if you have your nose in a book all the time."

She held up her book, whose cover showed a galaxy of stars above a turquoise sea dotted with shiny mermaid tales. "There's plenty going on in here," she said.

We were silent for a few minutes as I drove toward Dogwood Hills. The only noise was Aslan's loud breathing and the flipping of pages. Summer didn't notice we were taking a different route than usual, but when I stopped the car in front of the house on

Sweet Gum Lane, she finally looked up from her book. She glanced around, taking in the unfamiliar street with the wide lawns and neat houses shaded by mature trees.

"Where are we?"

I took off my seat belt and turned to her. "This house is for sale," I said, gesturing at the charming home behind her. "I wanted us to take a look at it."

Summer turned to look at the house. "Does it have a yard for Aslan?"

Aslan pressed his nose to the window and wagged his short tail vigorously at the sound of his name.

"I haven't toured it yet, but online, there were pictures of a fenced yard. Want to check it out with me?"

Summer turned to face me, her blue eyes curious. "What if I don't like it?"

"Then we'll look at another house."

"You won't buy it if I don't like it?"

I thought about it for a moment. Was I going to let my nine-year-old daughter make decisions for me?

Yes. Yes, I was.

"If you don't like it, I won't buy it."

Summer chewed her lip. "What if Aslan doesn't like it?"

I laughed and patted Aslan on the back. I was pretty sure he would like it. Aslan had been returned to the shelter multiple times before we adopted him. I figured he was simply happy to have a forever home and wouldn't object to the location.

"If Aslan doesn't like it, I won't buy it."

"You promise?"

"I promise."

We got out of the car and walked up the sidewalk toward the house. Jitters vibrated through me as we approached the front porch.

"This was my favorite house on the street when I was growing up," I told my daughter. "There used to be a tire swing in that tree." I pointed at the oak tree straddling the property line. "But other than that, it looks exactly the same."

Summer tilted her head back to look at the upstairs windows. "Do you think the bedrooms are upstairs?"

I walked up the wide front steps to the porch, where a swing hung from the rafters. "We'll find out in a minute."

I'd spent years imagining what the house would look like inside, and I was nervous it wouldn't live up to my expectations. Nothing else about my life had turned out as I'd planned. But I still had a faint glimmer of hope that some of my dreams could come true.

I pushed the doorbell, and a moment later, the door swung open. The real estate agent smiled and beckoned us inside.

"I'm Sarah," she said. "You must be Summer and Aslan."

I'd cleared Aslan with Sarah first, and she'd assured me as long as he was on his leash and house-trained, he was welcome.

Sarah smiled at Summer. "Do you go to Pinewood Elementary?"

"Yes, ma'am."

"Then you'll know a lot of kids in the neighborhood." She gestured behind her, inviting us inside, where sunlight streamed through the windows and the scent of freshly baked cookies hung in the air. "I can show you around, or you can wander on your own. Which would you prefer?"

I glanced around the open-concept living room and kitchen. The owners had decorated the space with soft lighting, warm colors, and a vintage rug. Family photos lined the walls beside mountain landscapes, and a stone fireplace anchored the far wall.

"I think we'll just wander on our own, if you don't mind," I said.

"Perfect. I'll be in the kitchen if you have any questions." She wiggled her eyebrows. "I've got chocolate chip cookies if you'd like one."

Summer's head lifted to me. "Can I have one, Mom?"

I usually didn't allow dessert before dinner, but since this was possibly a momentous occasion, I relented. "Sure, go ahead."

While Summer followed Sarah into the kitchen, I took a long look around. I'd been worried the interior wouldn't live up to my expectations for nothing. Excitement shivered down my spine as I took in the cozy reading nook, the built-in shelves, and the tall windows.

"Can we see upstairs?" Summer asked, munching her cookie.

"Lead the way," I said.

I followed my daughter up the stairs to the second story, where more photos decorated the hall, and a chandelier cast twinkling lights onto the gleaming oak floors.

There were three bedrooms, including a main suite with a spa bathroom, and a small office.

"Do you like it?" I asked Summer, joining her in the red, white, and blue-themed bedroom with bunk beds.

"Can this be my room?" she asked.

I took that as a yes. "Sure. We can repaint."

"Why? I like it like this. And the tiny window is so cute."

In addition to two large windows, there was a small round window overlooking the backyard that gave the room a whimsical flair. "Look," I said, pointing into the woods behind the house. "A tree house."

Summer leaned forward and peered out the window. "I never had a tree house before."

I smiled down at her. This was the house for us. I knew it in my bones.

We headed downstairs, where Sarah showed us the renovated kitchen, complete with modern appliances.

While Summer took Aslan outside to explore, I stayed behind to talk to Sarah. Glancing out the window at the yard next door, I noticed it was a mess of weeds and rusting lawn furniture.

"Does the grumpy old guy still live next door?"

"Mr. Pony?" Sarah asked.

I raised a brow. "Was that his name?"

"That's just what the kids called him because he always gave them rides on his back."

I frowned, unable to believe the grouchy man who'd yelled at me to slow down was the same man who was kind to children.

"Unfortunately, he passed away." Sarah shifted forward to look out the window into the neighboring backyard. "His nephew is renovating the house." She glanced down at my left hand and noted my lack of jewelry, then flashed me a smile. "He's single."

My muscles clenched at the thought of dating. Men were definitely not on my to-do list. I couldn't even bring myself to accept a date for drinks with a man I was incredibly attracted to. I didn't have time or the inclination for a man in my life. Plus, I had little to offer.

Sarah stared out the window with a wistful expression. "Now that the weather is warming up, he's often outside. Shirtless."

I rolled my eyes. "I'm not interested in the man," I said. "But I am interested in the house. Let's talk about the price. Is it negotiable?"

Sarah's eyes lit up. "What did you have in mind?"

Seven

For the last year, I'd been renovating my uncle's house room by room. I'd finished most of the house, including the kitchen, the living room, and the main suite, but I'd purposefully avoided Uncle Pete's office because it was just too damn painful.

Pete had been my dad's only brother. After my dad died, Pete had been the closest thing to a father figure I had left. Since Pete had a horrible relationship with his own children, I'd been the closest thing he had to a son.

Renovating his office brought up painful memories, and every time I tried to do it, I stopped and started another room.

I was officially out of rooms and had no excuses to keep me from ripping apart Pete's private sanctuary.

Armed with my tool belt and protective goggles, I entered Pete's office. It was a small room off the entry of the traditional-style house with a fireplace, built-in bookshelves, and two large windows covered in heavy velvet curtains. The walls were painted a mustard yellow.

When I'd visited Pete as a child, we'd been forbidden to enter his office. He didn't want us messing with his first-edition books or getting into his secret stash of whiskey.

So, it was the first place we hid during a game of hide-and-seek, and more than a few sips had been snuck from the whiskey. I'd stolen a kiss with one of my distant cousins during a Thanksgiving visit. I could still remember pressing her against the bookshelf and copping a quick feel while the old people lingered over pecan pie and coffee.

It was going to be hard to clear Pete's office, but luckily, I had reinforcements. Lacey arrived first, bringing a six-pack of my favorite craft beer and a rawhide bone to keep Daisy occupied.

"Again with the swim mask?" she asked, pointing to the mask dangling around my neck.

I took a beer and unscrewed the cap. "Gotta protect my vital organs," I said, taking a sip.

Lacey's eyebrows rose as she lifted her beer to her mouth. "You're the only man who can talk about your organ without sounding gross."

"My eyes, Lacey." I crossed my arms over my chest, sweeping my gaze around the room. I could hardly bring myself to touch anything. "Where do you think we should start?"

Lacey plopped down in the leather chair behind the desk and crossed her combat boots on the desk. "How about let's start with you telling me what happened the other night with Pressly?"

I swallowed roughly. "What?"

Lacey tipped her beer at me before sipping. "Tell me before everyone else gets here."

I walked over to the wall and pulled a worn copy of Shakespeare's *Hamlet* from the shelf. Pete had loved the old bard. "There's nothing to tell."

"You are such a liar. I could feel the tension all the way from the register."

I flipped through the pages, trying not to cough at the smell of mold escaping. "We weren't arguing."

"You really need to do something bigger to make up for breaking her heart."

I was saved from further discussion by the slamming of the front door.

Mia burst into the office, followed by Jay.

"I thought it was just us girls tonight." Mia glared at Jay.

"Are you calling me a girl?" I asked.

Mia planted her hands on her hips. "You know what I mean."

"I can leave if I'm unwanted." Jay scowled at Mia.

Tension filled the room as Jay and Mia squared off against each other, both of them carrying bottles of wine, neither of them backing down. Whenever the two of them were in the same room, sparks flew.

Lacey and I exchanged a look, and I crossed the room to put myself in between Jay and Mia. Jay was tall and broad, a former heavyweight champion, but out of the two of them, I thought Mia was more dangerous. She was tiny but mighty and known to carry mace.

"Play nice," I said. "Or you won't get dinner." I took the wine bottles from them and went into the kitchen. "Who wants wine?"

"Me," Jay and Mia said in unison.

I chuckled and inspected the bottles, guessing it was a safe bet to open both of them. After pouring a glass from each bottle and putting the beer in the fridge, I went back to my office.

Mia sat on the desk next to Lacey's booted feet, and Jay leaned against the opposite wall, staring broodily out the window.

One of these days, I would get to the bottom of why the two of them couldn't stand being in the same room together, but it wasn't today.

I gave Jay his wine, briefly considering switching the glasses before deciding it wasn't worth messing with them.

"Just so we're clear—" Mia accepted her wine and shot a glare in Jay's direction. "he's not in the book club."

Jay put his glass down on the shelf and selected a book. He flipped through the pages, then shut the book quickly, causing a cloud of dust to escape. He scrunched up his nose and replaced the book on the shelf. "Who said I wanted to be in your book club, anyway?"

Mia scoffed. "Do you even read?"

Jay shot her a look and crossed his arms over his chest, causing his impressive biceps to bulge. Before he could respond, the front door opened, and Sloane's voice rang out.

"Honey, I'm home!" She sailed by the office, her arms laden with take out bags. "A little help?"

I grabbed one of the bags and dipped my head to inhale the spicy aroma of Italian herbs. "Eat first?" I asked.

We headed into the kitchen, where I grabbed paper plates and Sloane unpacked the food. "Wait until you try the chicken parm," she said. "The new chef is amazing. He's a total dick, but boy, can he cook." She eyed the goggles around my neck, giggling. "Are you going swimming?"

I pulled the goggles off and tossed them on the kitchen counter. "Jesus. They're for the dust, okay? You have no idea what we're about to get into."

Everyone laughed, but they weren't laughing later when we were covered with dust.

"Wish you had these now, don't you?" I asked, peering at Lacey and Sloane through my goggles as we waded through piles of books that hadn't been touched in decades.

Lacey coughed and wiped her forehead with a bandana. "Next time, I'm gonna need more than delicious Italian food. I'm gonna grab another beer. Want one?"

"Sure."

"I need another helping of tiramisu," Sloane said, following her to the kitchen.

Jay and Mia had gone outside on a trash run. I could see them through the window, arguing over something as they carried bags full of things that had once been important to Uncle Pete.

God, I missed the old man. Sometimes I felt like he was still there, and if I glanced out the window, I'd see him sitting on the front porch, yelling at the cars to slow down.

He'd been a compact man with a headful of white hair and a face full of wrinkles. Stern and gruff on the outside, he'd been a marshmallow on the inside.

It was too bad my cousins were such pricks. They'd been manipulated by their mother into thinking Pete was a bad guy, but they'd never given him a chance. They'd moved to New York with her when she'd remarried and hardly spoken to him again.

It wasn't until he'd passed away that they'd tried to come around again. But by then, it was too late. Pete was gone, and they'd never have the chance to know their dad.

They weren't happy he'd left everything he'd owned to me.

Not that I'd wanted an outdated bookstore and a crumbling Victorian home in a neighborhood more suited to middle-class families than confirmed bachelors. I'd made the most of my inheritance, turning Hyperbole's into a thriving bookstore and renovating the house until it matched the others on the street.

Tearing my gaze away from the front porch, I climbed the ladder to reach the highest shelf on the bookcase and grabbed the last of the books. Sliding the last book off the shelf, I dislodged a large manilla envelope. I tried to grab it, but I wasn't quick enough. It slid off the shelf and landed with a solid thump on the floor.

A name was printed on the envelope in my uncle's neat handwriting. I pulled off the goggles and let them hang around my neck, peering down at the thick envelope. My heart slammed against my ribs as I made out the name.

Peppy Vinroot.

I scrambled down the ladder and grabbed the envelope. There could only be one reason her name was on that envelope—the letters.

I picked up the envelope, feeling the heft of it like a dead weight. Laughter sounded from down the hall, but it was just background noise compared to the thunderous slam of my pulse between my ears.

I pried open the envelope and reached inside, pulling out a

sealed envelope addressed to Peppy Vinroot, care of Pete Hayes. The familiar slant of my own handwriting transported me to a place that still gave me nightmares.

Panic paralyzed my body, but my brain spun into overdrive. Pressly had never gotten my letters. She'd never read my embarrassing confessions. She didn't know about the carnage I'd caused.

Sadness and relief warred in my chest as I stared at the letter. Uncle Pete had let me down by not delivering the letters to Pressly. But maybe he'd done me a favor. I pushed up from the ground, placing the letter back in the envelope with the others. A wave of dizziness crashed over me, but I reminded myself to breathe, and it passed just as quickly as it came up.

Lacey and Sloane came back into the office, with Mia and Jay close behind.

"You okay?" Lacey asked, peering up at me.

"You look like you've seen a ghost," Mia said.

My mind spun, but I managed a tight smile. The ghost I'd seen was me—the man I'd been before tragedy struck and changed my life forever.

December 2001

Dear Peppy,

I know you're probably super pissed at me right now, but let me explain. I didn't mean for this to happen. Standing you up was never part of my plan.

I thought we'd spend Thanksgiving together doing everything we've done before, but also catching up on your last year of high school and my first year of college.

By the time you see this letter, you will probably already hate me. But I hope I can change your mind.

I never had time to tell you how awesome you are. You're the girl every guy dreams of. Pretty, smart, and full of enough attitude to keep us guessing. I never thought a girl like you would be interested in someone like me.

Let's face it, I'm not exactly in your league. You could have any guy you want, but you picked me.

I know I took something precious from you. Something you can never get back. And I just want you to know how honored I am. How much I loved every fucking second we spent together this summer and I can't wait to see you again.

Whenever that may be.

Sincerely, Thatcher Hayes

Eight

I danced through the empty living room and into the kitchen, singing along to the Katy Perry song blaring through my headphones. It was our first night in our new home. As I slid along the bare, highly polished hardwood floors in my socks, I couldn't believe it was mine.

All mine.

It was a dream come true.

Not only had the owners accepted my offer, but they'd fast-tracked the closing. It had only been three weeks since the afternoon we'd toured the house, and we'd just moved in.

Although there were boxes everywhere and most of our furniture hadn't been delivered, it already felt like home. Summer's favorite—meatloaf—was in the oven, and the savory scent filled the air.

I was dirty and exhausted from carrying boxes, but not too tired to pirouette into the kitchen and pour myself a glass of wine. I was sipping happily, taking another appreciative look around my new home, when the ringtone I'd assigned to my ex sounded in my headphones.

A chill ran through me, and I took a long gulp from my glass before swiping a finger across the screen to answer, silencing "The Twilight Zone" theme song.

"Pressly Vinroot," I said in my most managerial tone.

There was a brief pause, and then Jeff's chuckle sounded. "I wondered how long it would take you to get rid of my name."

My spine stiffened, and I stared out the window into the backyard. Even if I was a far cry from the girl I used to be, Pressly Vinroot was my name. It might take me a while to feel like her again, but I planned to fake it until I made it.

"What can I do for you?" I asked, steering the conversation back on track.

"Is this an okay time?" he asked, putting on his best charming voice.

"What do you want, Jeff?"

"How have you been?" he asked in a soft voice that reminded me of early days together, when things had been fun and adventurous.

"We're great," I said, refusing to be swayed by the good old days. Not one part of me believed Jeff cared about how I'd been. He'd moved on from me long ago, and the only reason we had to talk was our daughter.

"I miss you," he said.

His voice sliced through me, and a wave of sadness washed over me. After watching my parents marry and divorce multiple times, I'd sworn it would never happen to me. But how was I to know I'd marry a cheating liar like Jeff?

"What do you want?" I asked again, affecting a bored tone.

He paused, and I could hear the sound of him sucking wind. It was something he did when he was anxious. "I want you to tell me you don't love me," he said. "Say the words, Pressly. Until you say them, I won't stop fighting for another chance."

My heart thundered in my chest, and tears swam in my eyes. This was nothing short of cruelty. Did I love Jeff? No. Of course I didn't love Jeff. But saying those words out loud was a different story. I wasn't a monster.

Then I remembered who I was. I was Pressly Fucking Vinroot, and she didn't let anyone walk on her.

"I've got dinner cooking, so if you didn't call for any particular reason, I have to go." I checked on the meatloaf, which was browning nicely, as if I had nothing better to do. "I'll see you next Friday when you come to get Summer."

They were having their monthly visit. Jeff was flying to Mossy Oak to get her, and they were flying back to Atlanta together for the weekend. I envied Jeff the uninterrupted time with Summer when all he had to do was be the fun parent. He got to do the skiing and the concerts while I was the one who grounded her and made her eat her veggies.

"I need to talk to you about that," Jeff said.

With a familiar sense of foreboding, I paced across the kitchen. Jeff had canceled their visit last month, saying he had a cousin's wedding in Turks and Caicos to attend and no children were allowed. "You're not canceling again?"

"Sorry, babe." His voice trailed off, sounding distracted. "I have to be at this fundraiser."

The background noise increased, and I pictured Jeff on a rooftop bar overlooking downtown Atlanta. I wished he was in the same room as me so I could punch him in the gut. Summer was going to be devastated, and I had to be the one to tell her.

"You're an asshole," I said.

"Don't call me that. You know I can't help it. Being a Carleton comes with obligations I can't skip out on."

The tears in my eyes threatened to spill, but I blinked them back and glared out the window into the backyard. Aslan ran around the perimeter of the yard, happily chasing a squirrel. I stared at him for a long moment, coming to terms with another disappointment courtesy of Jeff Carleton.

"Next week, then?" I asked, ready to be done with the conversation.

"Next week," Jeff said, the relief in his voice clear.

We hung up, and I downed the rest of my wine before trudging up the stairs to let Summer know her dad had canceled. Again.

Nine

I'd been avoiding Pete's office since I found the letters, but I could feel them in every room of the house. I'd probably read *The Tell-Tale Heart* too many times as a teenager, but I swore I could hear those letters throbbing with accusation as if they belonged in an Edgar Allen Poe story.

I couldn't avoid the office forever. It was the last room in the house to be renovated before I put the place up for sale.

My therapist would say I was intentionally stretching out the renovations so I didn't have to sell the place.

Fuck therapy.

It hadn't worked for me.

Blabbing on about my guilty conscience did nothing to banish the nightmares or ward off the crippling anxiety that sprang on me out of nowhere.

What did help was reading. I could get lost in a book for hours and forget what a shitty human I'd been. Another thing that helped was boxing.

I'd found boxing in the army. It was something we did to pass the time when it seemed like all we did was wait. We didn't have equipment, but we had rules. No hitting below the belt. No hitting an opponent when he was down.

Fighting was more entertaining than cards and kept us active when we thought we'd die of boredom.

When I'd come back to the United States, I'd continued boxing. After a few years of competing in amateur matches, I had a short stint as a pro. My record was decent, but I'd never cared about the wins. I got in the ring for the same reason I opened a book. I wanted to get lost for a while.

I was done with professional boxing, but I still trained like I was getting ready for a match. After spending the day at the bookstore, I headed to Out of the Box and put in a workout that would hopefully make me too tired to think about those letters in Pete's desk drawer.

"Hey, Thatcher!"

I turned away from the punching bag and saw Jay beckoning me from the ring. Wiping the sweat from my face with a towel, I headed over to join him and Manny.

"You got time to spar tonight?" Jay asked. "Manny needs a partner."

After a quick check on Daisy, who lounged behind the receptionist's desk, getting extra attention from Tracey, I grabbed my gear and climbed into the ring.

We traded punches for a few minutes while Jay watched and gave his advice. "You're gonna need to be quick on your feet. If he gets a solid punch on you, it could be over before it starts."

Manny glared at Jay, and I could see what he was thinking. There was no way the Hitman was getting a lucky punch on him. Manny was too prepared.

He danced lightly on his feet, throwing a solid left at me. I ducked, and he threw a quick right, which I blocked with my glove.

"Fuck!" Manny groaned and clutched his hand, his face crumpling with pain.

"What happened?" Jay stepped into the ring, reaching for Manny's right hand.

"I don't know." Manny grimaced as Jay pulled off his glove

and inspected his hand. "Felt this crack, and now it hurts like a motherfucker."

A sinking feeling landed in my gut. Manny couldn't make a fist without groaning.

"Shit." Manny tore off his headgear and threw it to the canvas. "It's broken. I know it."

"Calm down," Jay said, his face pinched with concern. "We'll get an X-ray before we start panicking."

"I'll grab some ice." Ducking under the ropes, I jogged off toward the ice machine.

By the time I got back with a bag of ice for Manny's hand, half the gym had circled the ring. The smell of sweat tinged with fear filled the air. Everyone in the gym knew what it meant if Manny was hurt. Out of the Box needed Fight Night to happen. The event had grown to include several amateur fighters and a debut pro, but the showdown between Manny "Killer Bee" Perez and "The Hitman" Logan Malone was the main card.

Jay grabbed the ice from me and pressed it to Manny's injured hand. The look he gave me confirmed my fears. We didn't need an X-ray. We both knew it was broken.

Guilt sat like a fifty-pound weight on my chest as I showered and drove home. I tried to remind myself that shit happened when you hit things, but I still felt responsible for Manny's injury.

If I hadn't have blocked his punch, he wouldn't be sitting in the emergency room right now. If I hadn't had time to spar, maybe none of it would have happened.

I turned onto my street and saw that every light was ablaze in the house next door. When I'd left that morning for the bookstore, there had been a moving van in the driveway. A figure moved past the window, and I looked away, determined not to be nosey. We had Chelsea Taylor in the neighborhood for that. The woman knew everything that went on in Dogwood Hills and prided herself on spreading the news.

Parking my Jeep in the driveway, I let myself in through the side door so I didn't have to walk by Pete's office. Daisy ran into the backyard through her doggie door, and a moment later, I heard the sound of excited barking. The neighbors had a friendly dog from the sound of it. Hopefully, they were half as nice as the former owners.

I grabbed a beer from the fridge and contemplated the meager offerings for dinner. My appetite was gone thanks to Manny and his broken hand, so I grabbed a beer instead.

Jay was just building up a reputation, and it would be devastating to cancel Fight Night. Champion's Corner depended on the money to keep going. Half the kids were on scholarships.

I remembered what it had been like being one of those kids who never had enough money. My parents had worked hard, but we weren't rich. I'd never have been able to join a program like Champion's Corner without a scholarship.

Sinking onto a barstool, I twisted off the bottle cap and gulped a long sip of beer. Daisy burst into the kitchen from the dog door and dashed by me. A scrap of fabric hung from her mouth, dragging on the floor as she raced through the kitchen.

"Daisy! Whatchu got, girl?"

She ignored me and bounded up the stairs. I followed, taking the stairs as fast as my tired legs would allow. Each step reminded me of the punishing workouts I'd been doing for the last week since I'd found those fucking letters addressed to Peppy Vinroot.

The double doors at the top of the stairs were open to the main bedroom, and I could see Daisy wiggling herself under the king-sized bed. I dropped down to my knees and stared at her.

"Daisy! Leave it!"

The command worked like a charm, and Daisy abandoned her treasure and crawled out from under the bed. When she hung her golden head and looked up at me with remorseful brown eyes, I didn't have the heart to scold her. I stroked a reassuring hand down her silky back. She gave my face a lick, and all was forgiven between us.

I reached under the bed and grabbed what Daisy had been hiding.

It was a lacy cupped bra for a woman with the perfect handful. Daisy must have stolen it from next door.

I must have been truly exhausted, not to mention sex-starved, because I felt like a teenager again, getting a glimpse at a Victoria's Secret catalog stuck between the flyers in the mailbox. A bolt of desire shot through me as I pictured the woman who wore this bra. It was practical but, at the same time, so fucking sexy.

Did she have a matching set of panties? Maybe with a little bow above the triangle of her thighs?

Jesus. I shoved a hand through my damp hair.

I needed to get laid.

The doorbell rang, interrupting my dirty fantasies. I could only hope it wasn't the owner of the bra or, worse, her husband.

Daisy barked and ran to the stairs. It took me a little longer to get to my feet and make my way to the door. My muscles screamed in protest with every move I made, and the stiffness in my pants refused to give up the idea of my sexy new neighbor.

"Daisy," I said in a firm command. "Sit." She sat obediently and looked up at me for praise. "Good girl."

I opened the door, but no one was there.

A delivery bag of food was on my front step. A car peeled away from the curb as I bent down to grab the bag. A receipt from the Hungry Panda stapled to the top of the bag had my neighbor's address at the top.

Shit. The delivery driver had messed up, and now it looked like I had no choice but to meet my new neighbors.

Shoving the image of the stolen bra out of my mind, I walked next door and rang the doorbell. As I waited for it to open, I steeled myself to meet the owner of the sexy bra, but when the door opened, I got something much better—Peppy Vinroot.

She blinked up at me with an adorably confused expression. "Thatcher? What are you doing here?"

I offered up the delivery bag. "I think this is your food," I said, hardly believing my good fortune. "I live next door."

My gaze drifted down her body. She wore a T-shirt knotted at her waist and black leggings. What did she have on underneath?

Heat filled my chest as I pictured her in a bra like Daisy had stolen and matching panties—because a woman as put together as Pressly would obviously wear a matching set.

Then, I noticed a wisp of smoke clinging to the ceiling in her living room, and the scorched smell of fire hit my nose. "Is something burning?" I asked.

Ten

Electricity tingled through me as I opened the door. I leaned against the doorframe, drinking in the sight of Thatcher Hayes.

I'd expected the delivery guy from the local Chinese restaurant, but he was much more appetizing. His damp hair was brushed back from his face, and he smelled fresh from the shower.

Every muscle in my body went weak, and memories crashed over me like waves. I remembered the soft brush of his hair against my cheek, the fullness of his mouth as he coaxed my lips open to sweep his tongue inside, the hardness of his body.

Exhaustion, too much wine on an empty stomach, and Jeff's assholery had numbed my brain. I didn't realize I was staring until Thatcher waved his hand at me.

"Is everything okay?" His blue eyes were wide with concern. "I smell smoke."

I snapped back to the present and straightened from the doorframe. "It's fine. Wait." My heart hammered hard in my chest, and suddenly, it was very hard to breathe. "Did you say you were my neighbor?"

He glanced at the house next door, then turned back to me with a panty-melting smile. "Looks that way."

I leaned against the door again, feeling like I might pass out.

"You sure you're okay?" Thatcher asked, concern pulling his brows together. "I think something is burning."

My vision blurred, and my chest heaved as I dragged in a breath. I'd never had an anxiety attack before, but I was pretty sure that was what was happening. I tried to push away from the doorframe, but I wobbled on my feet.

"Whoa." Thatcher dropped the delivery bag and reached out to catch me. "Easy there."

I melted into his warm embrace, letting his strong body take my weight. It felt so damn good to lean on someone, especially when he felt as sturdy as a brick wall and fully capable of supporting me.

Sweat broke out on my forehead, and a chill passed over my skin. He smoothed my hair back from my forehead and smiled down at me. "I've got you," he said.

And so he did. He cinched me tightly to his chest, his arms as strong as an oak. I could feel the steady pulse of his heart against my cheek and smell his masculine scent. His blue eyes locked on mine, searching for answers, probing so deeply I felt suddenly shy.

Finding my strength, I pushed out of his arms and took a step back. "Sorry. I guess I had too much wine on an empty stomach."

His tongue pushed against the inside of his cheek as he evaluated me with his intense blue stare. "Thank fuck for delivery," he said.

I smiled, glad he'd let my near fainting episode drop without a fuss.

"I burned dinner," I said.

Stupid Jeff. He'd made me lose track of time as I was breaking the news of his cancellation to Summer. She'd been so upset I'd ended up staying with her and helping her unpack her books. Then we'd made her bed with the comfy quilt and plush pillows she'd picked out on her own.

When the smoke alarm had gone off, I'd raced down the stairs, but it was too late to save the meatloaf. Instead of Summer's favorite home-cooked meal, we were going to have Chinese take out.

"Mr. T?" Summer's voice sounded from behind me. "Are you the delivery man?"

Thatcher bent to pet Aslan, who was never far from Summer. "Nah," he said. "I'm your neighbor."

She giggled, and the sound sent a rush of happiness through my entire body. Summer was a different kid around Thatcher. Not only did she come out of her shell, but she was actually nice. Her smile was like a ray of sunshine on a dreary day, and her hunched posture straightened.

"Can Mr. T eat with us?"

Gone were the tears she'd cried after finding out her dad wasn't coming to get her. She was as happy as I'd ever seen her.

Thatcher pinned me with a look, and unspoken words flew between us. We were neighbors now, and I was going to have to get used to seeing him on a daily basis. For years, I'd cast him as the villain, but now that we were face-to-face, I had a hard time remembering his faults.

All I could remember was the way he'd looked at me as if I was the only girl in the world. Just like he was looking at me now.

But we weren't teenagers anymore.

I wasn't the sassy girl so full of confidence I'd once been. Maybe the chemistry I felt from Thatcher was all one-sided.

"I'm sure Thatcher has dinner plans," I said.

A small smile lifted his lips. "Actually, I'm free. If you'll have me, I'd love to help you eat all this." He hefted the bag, which had enough food to feed half the block. "Hopefully, you got extra egg rolls?"

Summer grabbed the bag and let out a squeal of delight. "Mom always gets extra egg rolls."

She ran off into the kitchen, but Thatcher stayed put, his gaze finding mine. "Can I come in?"

His voice was a quiet caress, sending tingles all over my body.

Warmth raced from my chest to my face, and I prayed Thatcher didn't notice the blush on my cheeks. A rush of desire pulsed through me, and I felt parts of me come alive for the first time in years.

I took a step back and invited him in.

<hr>

Eleven

"How do you like your new house so far?" I asked.

"The sink's broken," Summer announced. "Mom tried to turn it on, and nothing happened."

I pushed up my sleeves. "I can take a look at that. I'm pretty handy."

Pressly busied herself with the take out bags. "No need," she said. "I'll call a plumber."

A grin curved my mouth. "What are neighbors for?"

She gave me a flirty look that went straight to my cock before clearing her expression. "If you insist."

The first thing I did was try the handle. When nothing happened, I bent and reached under the sink. "Did you try the supply valve?" I asked.

"What?"

I twisted around and saw Peppy staring at my ass. Busted. She may be prickly with me, but there was nothing wrong with our chemistry. It hadn't fizzled with the years. Instead, it had grown stronger and zinged between us like trapped lightning.

I smiled up at her, not minding the view from below. The little swatch of skin revealed between her knotted T-shirt and the top of her leggings looked as soft as satin.

"The supply valve controls the water flow," I said, reaching under the sink to grasp the valve and turn it. "Try the faucet now."

"Don't worry if you can't fix it. I'll call the plumber."

"Just try it, Peppy."

Her eyebrow ticked up. "It's Pressly now."

"Sorry." I flashed a smile. "Slipped out. Pressly, can you try the faucet, please?"

She stepped over me and reached for the faucet. Her shirt lifted higher, and I made a mental note to offer more of my handyman services to my new neighbor. Hopefully, something else besides her kitchen faucet was broken.

The splash of water sounded, and she jumped back in surprise, nearly tripping over my legs. "You fixed it!"

It wasn't broken, just turned off, but I refrained from telling her that and spoiling the moment. I slowly rolled to my feet. My muscles screamed in protest, reminding me of the brutal work I'd been putting in at the gym in order to forget the woman who was now my next-door neighbor. "Told you I was handy."

She glanced down at my hands, blushing furiously. I could see her thoughts as clearly as if they were written on her face. We'd once been very good with our hands on each other.

"Mr. T? Do you like rice or noodles?"

I dragged my gaze away from Pressly. Summer was staring up at me, oblivious to the tension pulsing between me and her mother.

"Both," I said, stepping around Pressly to wash my hands.

"Where are we gonna sit?" asked Summer. "We don't have any furniture yet."

"We can have a picnic in the living room. It'll be fun." Pressly poured Summer a glass of water and turned to the fridge. "Would you like wine?" she asked, pulling out a bottle of white wine.

"Got any beer?"

She shook her head. "Sorry."

I shrugged. "Wine is good."

She poured two glasses and grabbed our plates, taking them into the living room to sit on the floor. Summer launched into a synopsis of the book she was reading, but I was only half listening. I'd never thought that morning when I'd watched the moving van pull up next door that I would get lucky enough to have Pressly as my neighbor. I smiled a little, thinking it would be much harder for her to avoid me now that we shared a property line.

I watched her when she wasn't looking, noticing how pretty she'd become. She'd always been cute, but now she was fucking beautiful. She wore no makeup, and her hair was piled high in a messy knot, but she was naturally gorgeous—the kind of woman who didn't have to try.

My gaze dropped over her body. Thanks to Daisy, I had a pretty good visual of what she was wearing beneath her clothes.

"I hate math," Summer said.

I chuckled, thankful for the distraction before I mentally undressed her mother. "Math sucks," I agreed. "But unfortunately, it's pretty useful."

Summer rolled her eyes. "I still hate it. It's worse than ballet."

"Ballet is good for you," Pressly said, twirling noodles on her fork. "It'll teach you discipline."

Summer groaned. "I hate discipline."

I took a bite of my egg roll and chewed while mother and daughter competed in a staring match over their plates.

"Discipline is a valuable skill," I said finally. "It's why I like to box."

Summer blinked away from her mother and looked at me. "I want to box."

"Summer," Pressly said with a small laugh. "Boxing isn't for little girls."

"Yes it is," she insisted. "Girls box at your gym, right, Mr. T?"

I had a bad feeling about interjecting myself in the conflict, but I nodded. "Yeah. Champion's Corner has about twelve girls."

Pressly narrowed her eyes at me. "Champion's Corner?"

"The kid's program at Out of the Box," I said. "Remember?"

"Mom never listens," Summer said, glowering at Pressly. "She said we would talk about it later, and we never did. She lied."

Pressly flinched. "I didn't lie," she said. "We just haven't had a chance to talk about it."

"You didn't even remember what it was," Summer said.

Pressly's gaze sought mine, pleading for backup.

I leaned back on my hands, trying to think of something to say to ease the tension. "We're getting pretty old," I said. "It's hard to remember everything. You're lucky you still have a few good years left, kid."

Summer turned her attention back to her food, and Pressly shook her head slightly at me. I shrugged. What did I know about kids? I only had Daisy to look out for, and she didn't talk back.

"Can I be excused?" Summer asked after an awkward silence.

Pressly bit back a sigh and nodded. "Sure, that's fine. I'll be up in a minute to tuck you in."

Summer's chin poked out. "I don't need you to tuck me in."

Pressly stiffened for a moment, then recovered quickly. "Okay. Brush your teeth. I'll come check on you in a few minutes."

Summer stood up and took her plate to the trash before starting up the stairs with Aslan on her heels. "Good night, Mr. T," she said. "I'm glad we're neighbors."

My heart warmed, and I glanced quickly at Pressly. "That makes two of us."

When Summer and Aslan had gone upstairs to bed, Pressly stood and carried her half-eaten plate to the trash. She glanced around her house, gaze tracking over the blank walls and empty rooms. "You're probably wishing the delivery guy wouldn't have messed up tonight," she said.

I joined her in the kitchen. "Of course not. I'm always happy to eat an egg roll from Hungry Panda."

The theme song for "The Twilight Zone" sounded from Pressly's phone on the kitchen counter. She glared at it but made no move to answer.

"Are you gonna get that?"

"I don't want to," she said. "But he won't stop calling until I answer."

I glanced at the phone and saw the screen light up with Jeff Carleton's name. "Your ex-husband?"

"Yeah. The douchebag just called and canceled his weekend with Summer. Wonder what he wants now?"

"Want me to find out?" I asked.

Humor sparked in her eyes. "He would flip out if a man answered my phone."

"Then let's make him flip out."

When she nodded, I grabbed her phone and swiped my thumb across the screen to answer.

"Hello?" I said in my best baritone.

Pressly giggled, stifling the sound with a hand clapped over her mouth.

There was silence on the other end of the phone, and then finally, a man's voice demanded, "Who's this?"

"Thatcher Hayes. Can I help you?"

Jeff cleared his throat. "I'm trying to reach Pressly Carleton."

"Sorry, she can't come to the phone right now." I held Pressly's gaze. The way she was looking at me made me feel like a goddamn hero. "Can I take a message?"

"Put my wife on the phone," Jeff said, his voice dripping with entitlement.

"Shit," I said, sounding shocked. "You're married, baby?"

There was a choking noise from Jeff on the phone, and Pressly burst into laughter. I grinned at her, feeling that familiar shift in my chest that I used to get every time I saw her.

"Just put her on the phone, buddy."

I met Pressly's gaze, and she shook her head vigorously. "Sorry, *buddy*. She doesn't want to talk to you."

"Listen to me, motherfucker," he said.

I hung up before he could continue. "Want me to turn your ringer off?"

Pressly nodded, still giggling.

"What an asshole," I said.

"You have no idea." Her laughter died away, and she took a step back. I felt the wall she put between us as clearly as if it was a physical barrier.

"Hey," I said, taking a step closer in an attempt to gain back the ground I'd fought so hard for. "I'm really sorry."

Her posture stiffened, and her eyes flashed to mine, twin blue pools of ice. "I appreciate you handling Jeff, but I don't need your sympathy."

Frustration mounted in my chest. "I wasn't talking about Jeff," I said. "I'm sorry I didn't show up on Thanksgiving."

Even though it was the truth, the words weren't quite right. The apology wasn't the important part. I needed to tell her the reason why I hadn't come.

"You didn't show up either?" she asked. "All these years, I've felt so much guilt about it. But I guess neither one of us cared enough to show up, right?"

It felt like she'd reached into my chest, grabbed my heart, and squeezed. "You didn't show?"

She shook her head, but she wouldn't meet my gaze. Something was off. She was holding back.

Taking a step closer, I placed my hands on the counter behind her and caged her in. Electricity sizzled between us. Being so close to Pressly made my senses go haywire. I could smell the floral scent of her shampoo and feel the tickle of her breath on my neck.

Time dragged on as our gazes clashed. My mind spun as I tried to rewrite the story that had been playing in my head for decades. For so long, I'd been eaten up with guilt, picturing Peppy on her dad's boat, waiting for me at the marina for hours before leaving with a shattered heart.

I'd been wrong.

Her hands came up between us, palms resting flat on my chest. But she didn't push me away. She spread her hands up my chest to my shoulders, a gentle pressure on my tight muscles. A shiver of anticipation rushed down my spine, and my blood ran south. My dick stirred to life, a painful ache to rival the one in my chest.

"I guess I was nothing to you, then?" I growled. "You were always too good for me."

"No. I wasn't."

"Yeah, you were, but I wanted you anyway."

She lifted her chin, bringing our faces so close together that I could have lowered my mouth an inch to kiss her. I didn't. The next move needed to be hers.

"Thatcher," she said.

I leaned closer, pressing my body against hers so she felt the hard bulge of my arousal. She pulled in a sharp breath, causing her breasts to rub against my chest.

"And now?" Her gaze locked on mine, a glimmer of temper shining in them. "Now I'm the poor divorceé next door in need of a handyman and a sympathy fuck?"

Her words cut deep, and I took a step back, dragging a hand through my hair. "That's not what I'm offering."

"Don't you dare feel sorry for me," she said.

Our eyes clashed and held. Heat pulsed between us, and the only sound was our labored breathing.

"Look, Peppy—"

"Don't fucking call me that ever again." Her temper snapped, and her eyes flashed. "I'm not that girl anymore."

"No, you're not." I thought of the girl I'd known with the perfectly charmed life. The girl who'd taken her privilege for granted. "You're someone better."

She gasped, and her eyes went wide. Two spots of color appeared on her pale cheeks.

The doorbell rang, the chime sounding so loudly in the silence it made us both jump. Pressly scrambled to the other side of the kitchen.

She cast a glance at the door, still breathing hard. "You should go."

Her dismissal hurt, but I'd experienced worse. Grabbing my jacket, I draped it over my arm. "I'll let myself out the back," I said.

She nodded and walked to the front door, her elegant posture giving away nothing of what had just transpired between us. The poised facade she showed the world was firmly back in place.

Our moment was over, and I wasn't sure when I'd get another. It had taken me months to get her to talk to me.

Exhaustion hit me like an iron fist as I trudged across the yard to my house.

I might not survive falling for Pressly Vinroot again.

February 2002

Dear Peppy,

People think war is scary, but really it's just boring. We sit around all day waiting for something to happen. Nothing happens.

Then we walk. We walk so much my feet are covered in blisters.

We walk. We sleep in the bush. We walk more.

The food is shit, but it's too hot here to eat anyway.

I don't know where I'll be tomorrow, but I know where I want to be.

With you.

Sincerely, Thatcher Hayes

P.S. If you get this soon, please send books. Anything fantasy or SciFi, but I like historical too.

P.S.S. And maybe send a picture too?

Twelve

I lied to Thatcher.

When I opened my mouth, I hadn't intended to lie, but it had just come out. He already thought of me as the victim of an asshole ex-husband. I didn't want him thinking I had sat around for hours waiting for him to come that night so long ago.

So, I'd lied. And now I feel horrible.

I *had* waited around for hours—he didn't need to know that. The only person who knew how pathetic I'd been, sitting on my dad's boat all alone with a broken heart, was me. And it was going to stay that way.

When Thatcher was gone, I opened my front door and saw Gabi Salinger standing on my porch. Her mouth dropped open, and she blinked up at me in surprise. "Pressly! I didn't know it was you who bought the house."

"Hi, Gabi," I said, stepping back to allow her inside. "Come in."

She came in and took a slow look around. "It's gorgeous in here," she said. "I've never been inside before."

She handed me the plastic container she was carrying. "I was gonna lie and say I made these, but I grabbed them from work.

Someone has been leaving treats in the break room, and I snagged these before anyone else could get to them." She lifted the lid and grinned. "Chocolate chip cookies."

I glanced down at them, barely registering the enchanting smell of chocolate. "You want wine?" I asked.

She cocked a brow at me. "Sure."

I opened another bottle of wine and poured two generous glasses. I was going to regret having so much wine tomorrow, but at the moment, I didn't care. Thatcher had pinned me against the counter and nearly kissed me. It was the most action I'd seen in two years, and I was more than a bit shook up about it.

We settled on the floor, sitting cross-legged with our wine and cookies.

"Welcome to the neighborhood." Gabi raised a glass to me. "Do you like it so far?"

I took a bite of the cookie, letting the chocolate melt on my tongue. "It's great."

"I'm so excited to have another single mom on the street."

I stiffened, still not used to my single status after having been married for so long. "I used to love this street as a kid," I said.

"Me too."

Gabi and I were about the same age, but we hadn't known each other when we were growing up. I'd been shipped off to boarding school at fourteen and only visited on holidays.

"Remember that mean old man next door?" I asked. "I guess that was Thatcher's uncle."

I hadn't meant to bring Thatcher up, but once I said his name, it hung heavy in the air. I couldn't believe I'd almost let him kiss me.

What had I been thinking?

I guess I hadn't been. What with the throbbing erection in his jeans pressing into me and the silk of his hair feathering against my cheek, it was no wonder I couldn't form a coherent thought.

Thank God for the doorbell, or else I would have easily done something I'd regret.

"I wonder why Thatcher didn't tell me you were moving in next door," Gabi said. "Seems like something he would have mentioned at book club meetings."

I'd forgotten Thatcher was the friendliest person in town. Everyone knew him and loved him. He was the knowledgeable bookstore owner, the volunteer for the kid's boxing team, and the esteemed Mr. February of the Men of Mossy Oak calendar.

"He didn't know," I said. "Neither of us did."

Gabi laughed. "You say that like you wouldn't have bought the house had you known."

I sipped my wine, polishing off my cookie. "Who knows?"

"This is going to make it very hard for you to continue to avoid each other."

"Who said we were avoiding each other?"

Gabi laughed. "This is a small town, remember? Everybody knows everything." She leaned closer. "I heard you knocked over a display of canned peas at Blanchard's trying to skirt away."

I straightened my shoulders. "Actually, it was corn." I wrinkled my nose in disgust. Creamed corn."

"Guess you guys can't avoid each other anymore."

"I have no interest in dating right now. Especially Thatcher."

Gabi shrugged. "I know you guys have a history, but try to give him a break. Thatcher isn't like other guys."

"How do you mean?"

"He's in a book club with five women," she said.

I shrugged. "Sounds like something a horny guy would do."

Gabi laughed. "Not Thatcher." She shook her head. "He's got a good heart."

I clenched my jaw. "Why don't you go for him, then?"

"No way. He's not my type."

I raised my brows. How could a man like Thatcher, who was pure eye candy, not be someone's type? "So you don't think he's hot?"

"Oh, he's hot alright," she agreed. "But so is Beckett."

I threw up a little in my mouth, remembering the smell of his stinky socks. "Ugh. That's my brother."

"Exactly." She raised her wineglass in the air like I'd hit the nail on the head. "Thatcher is like my brother." She turned thoughtful and sipped her wine. "You know how I lost my husband, right?"

I nodded. Gabi had married young, and her husband had died while serving in the military. He'd never even known their son, Shane.

"Thatcher went through some serious shit in Sierra Leone. A lot of people he cared about died. He understands."

I was struck numb. Sorrow for the boy I'd known filled my chest. Thatcher had been a kid on his way to college, his future a blank slate to fill. He'd been kind and chivalrous, the kind of boy who stood up to bullies and coached Little League in his spare time.

I'd practically begged him to take my virginity. And when he'd had, he'd been sweet and soulful, taking my heart along with everything else I had to offer.

"Have you seen the calendar yet?" Gabi asked.

My focus snapped back to the present. "What calendar?"

"The Men of Mossy Oak calendar?"

My mind drifted to the calendar hanging in my office. It was April, but I hadn't switched the page from February, because... Thatcher. Swoon-worthy Thatcher was the best of the twelve.

Gabi snorted with laughter. "You've definitely seen the calendar."

I turned wide, innocent eyes, and she laughed harder. "How did you know?"

"I have a fourteen-year-old son," she said. "I have a built-in lie detector. And you should see your face right now." She did a very accurate impersonation of my feigned innocence.

"Shut up. I bet you know how many macarons are on Fred's boxer briefs."

She collapsed into a fit of giggles. "I hear next year is gonna be even hotter," Gabi said. "They've got a firefighter lined up, and that sexy owner of the boxing gym with the tattoos is gonna pose."

Boxing made me think of my neighbor again.

"How does such a small town have such a high population of gorgeous men?" she asked, smiling wistfully. "You should see the Spanish teacher at my school."

"They need to add that to the billboard when you enter town." I raised my hand like a marquis sign. "Mossy Oak Population 7,744. Plenty of hot men."

We dissolved into laughter, and I felt like I was truly home. It had been a long time since I'd drunk wine and eaten cookies with a friend.

"You're really not into Thatcher?" Gabi asked on her way out.

The question stopped me in my tracks. I hadn't been ready to unpack my feelings for Thatcher since moving back to Mossy Oak, but now it looked like I didn't have a choice.

"I don't know," I said.

Gabi stepped out onto the porch. "I guess you'll find out as soon as you see him bring a woman home."

What a cruel twist of fate to have my dream house placed next door to the first man who'd broken my heart.

Thirteen

Manny's hand was broken.

Fight Night was in danger of being canceled, which could lead to the downfall of the gym.

Since it was partly my fault, there was no way I could let it happen. There was only one thing to do. I had to fight.

I'd tell Jay in the morning.

With the decision made, I tried to focus on my book. It was a very entertaining historical fiction book that should have held my attention, but my mind kept straying. Between my decision to fight, my new neighbor, and the letters in Pete's office, my attention span was fucked.

I let my book fall to the coffee table and walked to the window. Moving aside the curtain, I peered at Pressly's house next door. Lights blazed inside, but the blinds were closed. I couldn't see a damn thing.

I let the curtain fall and stalked down the hall to Pete's office. From his window, I had a direct view of her driveway. There were no cars parked there, which meant she probably didn't have company.

Jesus Christ. I'd become a creepy stalker.

The first time I saw another man at her house, I was going to lose my mind.

I stepped away from the window and sank into the chair at Pete's desk. The letters I'd written were still in the drawer, pulsing with a Poe-ish life of their own.

I'd trusted Uncle Pete to get Pressly those letters, and he'd let me down. Or had he? Just how embarrassing were the letters? I couldn't remember what I'd written. I'd been a mess those first few months I'd joined the army. I'd just lost my dad, uprooted my life, and been sent into the African bush to fight a war most Americans didn't know existed.

I couldn't bring myself to open the letters. And I could hardly be angry at Pete, who'd left me his entire fortune.

Those letters didn't belong to me. They were addressed to the woman next door. If anyone should read them, it should be Pressly.

A knock sounded on my door, and I startled. I wasn't expecting anyone. Maybe it was the delivery guy again, bringing Pressly's food to my house by mistake.

The thought excited me more than it should have, and I hauled myself up from the chair to get the door. I pulled it open and saw Summer standing there with her trusty sidekick, Aslan.

"Hi," she said, staring at her feet.

"Hello," I said, glancing behind her and hoping for a glimpse of her mother. "Is your mom with you?"

Summer bent down to pet Daisy, who'd come, tail wagging, to the door. "No."

"Does she know you're here?"

Summer shrugged. "She's taking a bath."

The image of Pressly naked lodged in my mind. I shook it loose and focused on Summer. "What's up?"

She straightened and poked out her chin. "I was wondering if I could get your help."

Something tightened in my chest, and I realized I would move mountains for this little girl. Somehow, in the last few months, she'd crept into my heart and taken up residence. "Of course." Sensing she might need a little coaxing, I opened my door wider. "Want some hot chocolate?"

"I'm not supposed to have dessert so late. It's bad for my sleep."

I ushered her inside. "It'll be our little secret." In the kitchen, I rummaged through the upper cabinets, pulling down instant cocoa mix. "It's not nearly as good as the café's hot chocolate, but it's decent."

Summer sat down on the bench I'd built into the bay window and folded her hands in her lap, waiting patiently while I fixed her drink.

"How's school?"

"Okay."

I tried again. "And the new Percy book?"

Summer's face lit up. "I'm almost finished. I can't believe the Top Quester thought he could banish felines from the entire planet. What a dummy."

"Shhh." I covered my ears. "Don't spoil it for me."

"Sorry." She giggled.

When the milk was warm, I stirred in the mix and poured us both steaming mugs. "Careful, it's hot."

She raised a brow at me and glanced at the pot I'd just removed from the stove. "Yeah, I know." She blew on the surface. "I'm not a baby."

I sat down across from her and smiled. "Sorry. I don't know shit about kids."

She giggled again, and the sound made a floating sensation rise in my chest. "You're not supposed to say 'shit.'" She clapped a hand over her mouth, eyes going wide.

"Don't worry, I won't tell your mother."

She dropped her hand. "Promise?"

"Of course."

Summer stared down into her mug for so long I thought she'd changed her mind about getting my help.

Finally, she lifted her face to mine, her blue eyes sparkling. "I want to join Champion's Corner."

"Awesome." I raised my fist to bump hers. "You can do it online. Your mom just has to sign the waiver."

Summer frowned. "My mom won't even talk to me about it. I was hoping you could say something to her?"

"Summer," I said, using her real name for the first time in forever. "It's not my place."

Her face hardened. "You won't even try?"

I folded my hands on the table between us. "I don't think she'd listen to me."

"Maybe I can get my dad to sign the waiver. I'm seeing him this weekend."

My skin crawled at the mention of her dad. "No. It has to be your mom."

A flush rose up Summer's cheeks. "Why?"

"Because—"

"She doesn't care about me!"

"I bet she cares about you more than you realize."

"No, she doesn't!" She scrunched up her nose. "And she ruined my life by moving here."

Dealing with an upset nine-year-old wasn't part of my skill set, but I took a deep breath and tried my best. "Her job is here," I said. "Your uncle is here."

"But my dad isn't!" Tears sprang to her eyes. "And I want to join the program! You have to let me."

I leaned forward, pinning her with a gaze that I hoped seemed wise, even when I felt completely out of my league. "Your mother is in charge."

She blinked rapidly, holding back tears. "She won't let me do anything."

"She loves you more than anything in the world."

She blinked a few more times, and then her eyes went round. "You like her," she said. "You like her because she's pretty."

I couldn't deny it. Taking a sip of my hot chocolate, I stalled for time to gather my thoughts. Clearly, I was failing at this guidance thing, but I might as well jump in headfirst. "Yeah, I like her."

Tears swam in Summer's blue eyes. "You can't like her!"

I sucked in a breath, reminding myself to stay calm. My experience with kids was limited to those in the after-school program. It rarely got emotional during a training session, and I was completely out of my league.

"When you get older, you'll understand," I said.

It was the worst possible thing I could have said.

Summer jumped up from the table and raced out of the kitchen. "I hate you!"

"Summer!" I called, pushing back from the table.

"I never want to talk to you again!" She flung the words at me, calling for Aslan as she stormed to the door. He followed obediently, casting a forlorn look at Daisy on his way out.

"Hey!" I stopped Summer on the porch. "I'll talk to your mom about it, okay?"

Her shoulders hunched, and she hung her head. "Okay."

"But I can't guarantee anything."

She nodded. "Thanks."

I watched her walk across the yard, Aslan following like a silent shadow.

If only Summer realized I was the last person her mother was likely to listen to, she wouldn't have bothered asking.

On the bright side, at least I had another excuse to talk to my neighbor. I was fucking pathetic.

<h1 style="text-align:center">Fourteen</h1>

The jet sprays on the tub pulsed hot water over my tense muscles. It felt like heaven. I relaxed in the tub, forgetting the long day, the kid who was hardly speaking to me, and the mountain of housework waiting for me.

As the tension in my back eased, my thoughts drifted to the man next door. What was Thatcher doing right now? Was he home alone? Or maybe he had a woman over?

God, it was going to kill me to see a woman's car parked at his house overnight. Gabi was right. I would find out exactly how much I felt for my neighbor as soon as I witnessed a sexy sleepover.

Suddenly, the jets stopped, and my massage was over. I pressed the button on the tub, but nothing happened. Maybe it was a malfunction in the Jacuzzi system. Hell, what did I know about Jacuzzis? Or anything home related?

We'd lived in an upscale condo building with a doorman in Atlanta when Jeff and I had been married. There was an entire service team at our fingertips.

I pressed the button again, frustration ruining any benefits of the bath.

Since I'd moved in, the house had lost some of its glamour. I hadn't realized just how many things could be broken in an older home. The Realtor had assured me that the two-hundred-page inspection report was nothing unusual for a seventy-year-old home. I should have known something was up when the owners had requested an expedited closing, but I'd been blinded by love.

Now I was feeling the burn of an older home with too many problems to count. So far, the hall toilet was leaking, there was a moldy smell in the basement, and the oven was on the fritz. Add in the jetted tub malfunction, and I was beginning to think I'd bought a nightmare instead of a dream.

I climbed out of the tub and dried off. Slathering night cream on my face, I examined my latest wrinkles and cursed Thatcher for having been immune to the aging process. It wasn't fair that he looked even better than he had as a teenager.

And it definitely wasn't fair that he smelled so incredible or that he had a special bond with my daughter that included the use of nicknames.

I dressed in comfy sweats and brushed my teeth. It was still early enough for popcorn and a movie. If I could get Summer to join me, even better.

I knocked on her door, but she didn't answer. "Hey, Summer?" I pushed open the door, only to find her room empty.

Frustration mounted as I went down the stairs, but by the time I searched the kitchen and living room, full-on panic settled in. Then I noticed Aslan was gone, too.

"Aslan?" I called, my voice high-pitched with fear as I checked the backyard.

I grabbed my phone, but I wasn't sure who to call. She didn't have any friends, and Beckett was out of town. It was too soon to call the police; they would only tell me to wait. The only other person I could think of to call was Thatcher.

Pulling on my shoes, I grabbed a jacket and ran next door. It seemed to take forever before he opened the door. My mind jumped to every possible scenario, none of them good. By the time Thatcher came to the door, I was shaking.

"Summer is missing," I said.

His blue eyes went wide. "What? I just saw her."

Hope swelled in my chest. "When?"

"She was over here with Aslan." He paused and looked down, unable to meet my eyes. "She said you were in the bath."

"When I got out of the bath, she was gone." I nearly choked on the emotion welling in my chest. "Aslan, too."

Thatcher's arms came around me, pulling me into his embrace. "It's okay." His hands stroked up and down my back. "She was just here not thirty minutes ago. Daisy can find them." He tightened his arms around me. "She couldn't have gone far."

I leaned into him and breathed in the scent of his freshly washed T-shirt. A stolen moment of comfort washed over me. Throughout my marriage, it was me who handled the hard stuff with Summer. I went to the parent-teacher conferences and consoled her when her pet fish Mr. Diamond died. Jeff did the easy stuff. He booked vacations to the Bahamas, secured front-row concert tickets to Taylor Swift, and jetted Summer off to ski trips in the Alps.

Jeff should be here with me, handling this situation. Parenting with me. It was what I'd signed up for when I'd stood in front of five hundred people in Jeff's childhood church and promised to be his partner until the end of our lives. After growing up with divorced parents, I'd vowed to get married only once and stay that way, but it hadn't worked out how I'd hoped.

Jeff had never been there for us when we'd needed him. During our entire marriage, I'd been alone.

"We'll find her." Thatcher's voice was a low, comforting promise. He released me and grabbed a sweatshirt from the back of his sofa. "Daisy!" he called. "Want to go see Aslan?"

Daisy bounded across the room and stopped at Thatcher's feet. Her tail thumped on the gleaming hardwood floor, and her golden brown eyes held steady on his face.

"Go find Aslan." Thatcher opened the front door, and Daisy ran out into the night.

All my hopes were pinned on the golden retriever circling the yard with her nose to the ground. When she squatted to pee on a bush, my heart sank.

"This isn't going to work." I pulled my cell phone from my jacket pocket. "I'm calling the police."

Thatcher's hand settled on my shoulder. "Breathe," he said, his voice low and calm by my ear. "It helps."

I sucked in a breath and held it in my lungs, feeling like no amount of oxygen could save me from my spiraling thoughts of doom. I'd done my share of therapy and knew the language. But breathing didn't help when every sip of air was like sucking through a collapsed straw.

After a moment, I regained control, and Thatcher and I started after Daisy. His long-legged strides ate up the distance between our houses.

I'd turned on every light in my house, and it shone like a beacon in the dark night.

We skirted around the side of the house through the flower beds, following Daisy. Images of Summer as a baby and toddler flashed in my mind. She'd always been small for her age. She was painfully shy and barely spoke a word before she was three.

Jeff's mother had thought something was wrong with her development and wanted to have her tested, but I knew Summer was smarter than average. When she'd finally started speaking, it was in full sentences. She'd picked up Spanish from our house-keeper and could count to ten en Español. And she was funny. She could do a spot-on impression of anyone in our family.

After the divorce, Summer had turned inward. She'd buried herself in her bookshelf, pulling away from all her friends and neglecting the activities she'd once loved.

"She hates me," I said, nearly tripping over an overgrown root in my side yard.

Thatcher caught my arm and pulled me upright. "She doesn't hate you." His hand shifted to my elbow, guiding me through the dark yard in pursuit of Daisy.

"I've done everything wrong," I said. "I shouldn't have kept working. Jeff wanted me to stay at home with her, and we had the money." I shook my head, remembering the bitter arguments Jeff and I had over my right to a career. "But I didn't want to give up my work." I blew out a breath. "This is all my fault."

"That's bullshit." He took both my hands in his. "Summer's a great kid, and you're a great mom. Everything is going to be okay," he said. "You have to flip your mindset. Think positively."

I sighed. "Easy for you to say. It isn't your daughter missing."

"Summer's not missing," he said, nodding his head at the far corner of my yard. In the tree house, a narrow beam of light shined out of the window. "She's waiting to be found."

My breath rushed out of my lungs. I hadn't even thought to look in the tree house. I started off, but Thatcher caught my arm, stopping me.

"She wants to join Champion's Corner," he said.

My eyebrows rose. "What?"

"That's why she came over," he said. "She wanted me to talk to you about it."

I glanced over his shoulder at the treehouse. "I need to go."

He nodded once, his eyes still locked on mine. "Good luck."

I left Thatcher in the yard and hurried off to the path between the trees that led to the treehouse. Relief filled me with every step I took closer to my little girl, but my shoulders didn't unfurl from my ears until I climbed the ladder and saw her sitting under a blanket with a flashlight illuminating her book. Aslan was by her side, his eyes shining at me in the darkness.

"Hey, there."

Summer aimed the flashlight at me, then pointed it back at her book and flipped the page. "Hey."

My pulse rocketed, but I took a deep breath, holding in my frustration. "I was worried about you."

"Why?" she asked, sounding much older than a nine-year-old should. "I'm just reading."

"You can't just take off like that," I said, keeping my tone even while my heart slammed in my chest. "I thought something happened to you."

"I'm fine."

I took a breath and tried to keep calm. "I see that, but you need to ask permission before you come out here next time. I was scared to death."

She sighed. "You didn't even know I was gone."

"I was..." I shut my mouth mid-sentence. It did no good to try to argue.

When my eyes adjusted to the darkness, I picked my way over to her and settled on the floor, drawing my knees up to my chest. "Thatcher said you wanted to join Champion's Corner," I said.

She jerked upright. "He told you?"

"Yes."

There was a long silence, and the tree house buzzed with unsaid words.

Summer's eyes went wide in her small face. "Are you gonna marry him?" she demanded.

"What?" At first, I didn't know what she was talking about, and then I realized she meant Thatcher, and I felt my cheeks flame. Good thing it was dark in the treehouse. "No, Summer. We aren't getting married. Why would you think that?"

"But you like him," she said. "And he likes you."

I cleared my throat. "We're friends."

"He's my friend!" Tears clogged her voice. "You ruin everything. You drove Dad away, you brought us here, and now you're stealing my best friend."

My breath caught in my throat, and I shifted closer to Summer. There wasn't anything I could say to defend myself. I remembered how horrible I felt after my parents' divorce. It was like my life had been turned upside down.

"I know how you feel," I said, feeling tears prick my eyes. "It's hard when things change and you have no control over anything."

Tears slid down her cheeks and landed with a plop on her lap.

Aslan shifted closer to her, and she reached out to stroke a hand over his back.

"I want to box," she said.

I took a calming breath, but it didn't help. "Why?"

Her brows drew together. "Because I want to be a superhero."

"Superheroes aren't made in boxing rings."

"Yes, they are," she insisted. "They aren't scared of anything." She choked back a sob. "I don't want to be scared."

I put my hand on her shoulder and squeezed. "Superheroes are still scared," I said. "They are just brave enough to face what they're scared of."

She swallowed hard. "I want to be brave."

"You are, my love." I stroked her soft hair. "You are."

A sob escaped her throat. "I want to be."

I pulled her into my arms, and we clung to each other. "I'm so sorry, baby girl." I cried along with her. "I should have listened to you."

Summer rested her cheek on my shoulder, and I made my decision. I was going to let my daughter be a superhero.

Jay sat at his desk, staring at me like I'd lost my mind. He was a former heavyweight champion, and he still looked the part. His nose had been broken more than once, and one of his eyebrows was split by a thick scar. Big and muscular, he wore his hair in a no-nonsense style that reminded me of my military days. Tattoos peeked out from the sleeve of his short-sleeved shirt and climbed up the side of his neck.

"I'm serious," I said.

"You're too old," he said.

I peeked through the blinds, casting a gaze around the gym floor. It was filled with a bunch of weekend warriors who thought their tattoos made them fighters. "You got anybody better?" I asked.

Jay's brows pulled together over the steely glint in his eyes. "You're really serious, aren't you?"

"That's what I just said."

Jay crossed his arms over his chest. "No way, man. No fucking way."

"It's my fault Manny broke his hand."

"Bullshit," Jay said. "You just happened to be in the ring that day. It could have been anyone."

"But it was me." I strode across the room and placed my palms flat on Jay's desk. "Let me fix this."

Jay squinted up at me. "I can't let you fight again. Remember what happened last time?"

Of course I remembered. I'd gotten my ass beat. "I'll train harder this time."

"All the training in the world won't matter if you freeze up again and let someone take you down." Jay shook his head. "I can't let you do that again. You know it."

"So, you'd rather let the gym close."

"Than see you dead? Yeah. That's right." Jay shuffled papers on his desk. "You don't have to play the hero. The gym won't close if we cancel the main event."

"What about Champion's Corner? Will it survive?"

Jay grimaced, not meeting my gaze, and I had my answer.

"We have three weeks until the fight. Plenty of time for me to get ready. You know I can take this dude."

"They don't call him the Hitman for nothing," Jay said. "He's dangerous."

I clenched my jaw. "So am I."

Jay cocked his head at me. "You were," he agreed. "And then you got old."

"I'll train hard and smart. I'll beat him. And if I don't win, at least I will have given the crowd a good show."

Jay pinched the bridge of his nose between his thumb and index finger, and I knew I had him. Honestly, he had no other options.

"I can start today," I said. Even though it had been years since I'd fought, my blood was already humming with adrenaline.

Jay ran a hand through his hair. "Is this really what you want?"

I'd been thinking about it since the day Manny broke his hand, and I knew it was what I had to do. "I'm the only one who can save Fight Night," I said.

Jay snorted. "Careful. You sound like one of those arrogant fighters instead of a bookstore owner."

I looked him square in the eye. "You know it's true."

His head jerked in a nod. "Fine." He pushed his chair back and reached into his desk drawer. "Have a seat," he said.

My jaw clenched. "Why?"

He glared up at me. "Because if you're gonna do this, you're gonna do it right." He pointed to the chair. "Sit your ass down."

I glanced at the door, eager to train. "I need to get started."

Jay slapped a folder on top of the desk, chuckling. "Don't worry. You're gonna be training soon enough."

I eyed the folder on Jay's desk. It didn't look like the other plain manilla folders stacked all over the place in his messy office. It was navy blue with a shiny gold crown logo, and it looked expensive.

"What's that?"

"You remember Cassandra Darling?" he asked.

There weren't many women like Cassandra Darling. Nearly six feet tall with flawless skin and an abundance of cleavage, Cassandra was hard to forget. "The social media chic from Charlotte?"

"She owns a public relations company," he growled.

I grinned. "You seeing her?"

His eyes narrowed, shooting fire at me from across the desk. "No, man."

"Sorry. My bad."

"I'm helping her out with a job, and she's doing some press for Fight Night." He pushed the folder toward me. "You've gotta do a press release, a conference, and a photo shoot."

I felt a headache building behind my eyes. "All that?"

Jay scoffed. "Part of the deal, man. Still want to take Manny's place?"

The thought of doing a press conference and a photo shoot made me feel slightly nauseous. I knew from posing for the Men of Mossy Oak calendar how embarrassing it was to be in the spotlight. The lights, the camera, the fully clothed chick spraying my naked chest with oil—it was beyond humiliating.

But nothing was gonna stop me from this fight.

"I'm in," I said, leaning forward to shake Jay's hand.

He reached forward and wrapped his beefy hand around mine. "I hope you don't have plans today," he said. "Because we got shit to do."

A spark lit inside me at the thought of getting in the ring again. I loved every minute of the focused concentration during a round. "Let's roll."

"Wait." Jay motioned for me to sit back down. Leaning forward, he placed his elbows on his desk and pinned me with a serious expression. "We gotta talk about what happened last time."

Annoyance sparked in my chest. "Shit happens in the ring. You know that."

He frowned, lines deepening around his mouth. "It can't happen again."

A muscle ticked in my jaw. "It won't."

His gaze darkened, scrutinizing me harshly. "You sure?"

Sweat broke out on my forehead, and a hollow feeling spread through my chest. I locked eyes with Jay and nodded grimly. "I'm sure."

If Jay knew I was lying, he didn't let on. "Alright," he said. "I'll send you the links to all his fights. You gotta study everything about him."

"Ten-four."

His eyes roved over me. "Let's talk about your weight."

I sucked in my stomach. "What about it?"

"You're gonna have to cut."

"I'm a solid one-ninety."

His eyebrow lifted. "I need you at one-seventy-five."

"Fucking hell."

"No more pizza. No more beer."

I groaned, but he ignored me and pushed the folder in my direction.

"Call Cassandra and set something up." He walked to the door and yanked it open, casting his gaze around the gym floor. "Yo, Beckett," he said, lifting his hand. "Got time to spar?"

I got to my feet. "Sparring already?"

Jay crossed his arms over his chest and looked down his nose at me. I was over six feet, but Jay towered over pretty much everyone. "I need to see what you got before I can fix it."

My chin came up, and I met his gaze with as much confidence as I could muster. "There's nothing broken."

He grinned. "We'll see about that."

Sixteen

After we put all our furniture in place and hung our pictures on the walls, it seemed the house went through its own settling phase. It groaned and creaked, squeaked and sighed—getting used to its new residents.

The first night I spent by myself when Summer went to see Jeff, I could hardly sleep. The wind whistled through cracks in the windows, and the furnace ticked. I stayed up half the night listening to the noises, then bolted upright at the sound of something scratching on my window.

It turned out to be the branches of an oak, but I couldn't get back to sleep.

Summer was with Jeff, and I had the day off work with no plans. I should have been excited to have a rare day to myself. Since moving to Mossy Oak, I hadn't had any downtime. But the long weekend stretched ahead of me like a list of chores I didn't want to do.

Aslan whined, letting me know he needed to go out. I reluctantly rolled out of bed, grabbed my robe, and went downstairs to let him outside.

The days were warming up nicely, but the mornings and evenings were still frosty. A wisp of fog clung to the tops of the mountains in the distance, and the smell of fresh grass and blooming honeysuckles hung in the air.

The night sky twinkled with a thousand stars that seemed close enough to touch, and the moon was a perfect silver crescent. Sweet Gum Lane was silent except for the gentle rustling of leaves in the breeze.

Darkness cloaked most of the street, but a single light blazed in Thatcher's house next door.

A shiver ran down my spine at the thought of my neighbor. He'd been there for me and Summer in a way Jeff rarely had been.

I trusted him.

And I wanted him.

When he'd backed me up against the counter and almost kissed me, I'd almost let him. I could still feel the heat of him like a brand.

But what he'd said had stuck with me even more than his touch.

You're not the girl you used to be. You're someone better.

A cool breeze whipped through the yard, bringing goose bumps to my skin. The chilly air made me feel alive, and thinking of Thatcher made me feel brave. Like a superhero.

The spunky girl I'd been at seventeen was still part of me. She was buried deep underneath layers of disappointment and failure, but she was still there.

Aslan barked, the joyful sound sharp in the silence. He ran down the length of the fence, pressing his nose to the ground. A bark sounded from Thatcher's yard, and Aslan's tail wagged so hard it looked to be in danger of falling off.

I heard the sound of a door closing, and then Thatcher's voice called out to Daisy. Overcome with curiosity to see what Thatcher looked like so early in the morning, I climbed onto a chair on the patio and peered over the privacy fence into his yard.

His morning appearance did not disappoint. He looked adorable with messy hair and a scruffy beard, holding a mug that puffed steam into the chilly air. His feet were bare, and flannel pants hung low on his hips. I could see the outline of the muscles in his back under the thin material of his T-shirt.

The air left my lungs in a breathy sigh. Apparently, I had a weakness for men in flannel I hadn't known about until that moment.

Thatcher turned to look in my direction, and it was too late to duck. His eyes lit as he caught sight of me peering over the fence.

He lifted his hand in a casual wave. "Hey, Pressly."

I blushed from the roots of my hair to the tips of my toes. "Hi, Thatcher."

"Nice morning," he said, taking a sip from his mug.

"Exceptional." I tipped my head to look at the sky, which was just beginning to brighten with an orange glow.

"Want to climb down from that chair and join me for a cup of coffee?" he asked.

A flush crept up to my ears, and I tightened my robe around my chest.

What would SuperPeppy do? The answer came immediately to my mind. She wouldn't waste a moment.

A wave of uncertainty washed over me, and I froze. What if things ended worse than last time? What if I got my heart broken again? What if the second time around wasn't as good as the first?

I looked down to see Thatcher gazing up at me. His firm eye contact sent a thrill of anticipation down my spine. My nipples hardened into stiff peaks, pressing against the satin of my camisole, and desire throbbed in my core.

A slow, playful grin lifted his lips. "Or I can deliver?"

Tingles swept up my spine and danced along the back of my neck. What was I waiting for? The old me would have already been in Thatcher's backyard.

Heart clamoring in my chest, I dismounted from the chair as gracefully as possible and crossed to the fence that separated our yards. When I pushed open the gate, Thatcher was waiting for me.

His blue eyes sparkled with humor. "If you want cream or sugar, you'll have to bring your own," he said.

"I take it black."

He grinned down at me.

"What?"

"I like your hair like that."

Pleasure hummed through me. "I like yours, too."

He laughed and ran a hand through his messy hair. "I woke up like this," he said.

I followed him into the kitchen, immediately impressed. The sage-green walls, dark cabinets, and open shelves were modern and masculine, and the smell of fresh coffee welcomed me. I glanced into the living room, where a floor lamp cast a warm glow on the oversized furniture, plush pillows, and potted plants.

"Nice place," I said.

"Thanks. You should have seen it before. The carpet was grass green, and the walls were burgundy. It was like being trapped in a Christmas globe circa 1972." Thatcher poured a mug of coffee for me. "Have a seat." He gestured at the table built into the bay window.

"Did you build this?" I slid onto the bench seat.

"Yeah."

He carried the mugs to the table and joined me, sliding in close so our knees brushed. We were barely touching, and the slight nudge of our thighs was just enough to make me ache for more.

"Thanks for your help with Summer the other night," I said, sipping my coffee. "I don't know what I would have done without you."

He shrugged. "Daisy's the one who did the hard work."

"I signed Summer up for Champion's Corner," I said. "She'll start Monday."

His eyebrow lifted. "No more ballet?"

I shook my head. It was still a touchy subject. "I don't like that she's quitting ballet, but it seemed a small enough thing to make her happy. She's really excited to start."

"I'll be at the gym a lot more," he said. "I can keep an eye on her."

"Do you work with the kids?" I asked.

He nodded. "I do some other stuff, too. I teach self-defense classes, and I'll be training a lot in the next few weeks."

I let my gaze drift down his body with appreciation. "You keep in pretty good shape," I said.

He cleared his throat. "Yeah. Do you know about Fight Night?"

"No."

"It's an event coming up in a few weeks. There are a few amateur fights, some of the juniors from Champion's Corner will be getting their debut, and the main card is a middleweight fight." He shifted to face me, our knees brushing together. "I'll be fighting."

My belly quivered. "You?"

He placed his hand on top of mine. "The entire town will be there," he said, tracing a pattern on my fingers. "But it would mean a lot to me if you came."

His touch made me feel like I was falling under a spell. "I don't know," I said. "I don't like the idea of watching you fight."

His palm turned over, and he captured my fingers. "Why's that?" he asked.

I worried my lip between my teeth. "Because I care about you," I said.

My voice came out surprisingly calm for how fast my heart was racing. I could feel the warmth radiating from his body and smell the clean, soapy scent of his skin.

He toyed with my fingers, frowning. "I care about you, too." His brows, a few shades darker than his light brown hair, pulled together. "I have so many regrets."

My breath hitched. "I meant what I said. I don't want you feeling sorry for me."

His gaze pinned mine, hot and hungry. "It's you who should feel sorry for me," he said. "I've been hard for you for months."

My body throbbed in response to the low growl in his voice. I squeezed my thighs together, trying to ease the ache between my legs.

I reached up to frame his whiskered jaw. "I want you, too."

"I have to warn you," he said. "I want it all with you."

Desire raced through me, but fear was quick on its heels. I blinked slowly, pulling back a little. "I'm not sure what I can give you," I said.

His arm slipped around me, pulling me so close I was practically in his lap. "Can I take this?" He dipped his head and nibbled the corner of my mouth, bringing shivers to my skin.

A low moan escaped my mouth. "Yes, please."

The words were barely out of my mouth before he pulled me onto his lap and kissed me. His mouth was soft and firm and so hot I thought I might burst into flames. He took control of the kiss, coaxing my lips open with a possessive sweep of his tongue.

He tasted sweet and earthy like the rich black coffee. His beard scraped against my jaw as he angled his head, kissing me deeper, plunging his tongue into my mouth. His hands spread down my back, squeezing my hips and urging me closer against the huge bulge in his pants.

"See what you do to me?" he rasped against my mouth.

I ground against him, feeling sexier than I had in years. Possibly ever.

Why had I waited so long for this pleasure? I'd deprived myself because I was too afraid of getting hurt again, but it seemed silly now that Thatcher's rough hands parted my robe and slid up my bare thighs.

"Jesus," he said, sucking in a breath as he looked at me. "Is this what you wear to bed every night?" He shook his head as if he couldn't get enough of seeing me in my satin shorts and camisole.

While Thatcher had only improved with age, I hadn't been so lucky. I'd given birth and hadn't been one of those women who bounced back easily. Nerves flooded my senses as his hand slid under the strap of my camisole.

"Wait." I clutched his hand, stopping it over my heart.

He dragged his gaze up from my chest to my face. "What's wrong?"

"I'm not…"

"You're not what?" His brows furrowed in concern, and then he smiled knowingly. "You're not a seventeen-year-old virgin anymore?" He trailed his knuckles over my exposed skin, calling up goose bumps. "You're all grown up now. Thank fuck."

The growl in his voice sent a shiver through my entire body. My belly fluttered, and heat pulsed between my thighs.

From across the room, an alarm sounded, the high-pitched noise startling us.

"Shit," Thatcher grumbled, sliding out from the bench with me still in his arms. He set me down on my feet and planted a kiss on the corner of my mouth. "Let me turn that off."

He grabbed his phone and shut off the alarm, then tossed it on the counter. Running a hand through his hair, he dragged in a deep breath. "I'm sorry, but I have to go. I'm meeting Jay at six."

"I should go, too. Aslan is probably wondering where I got off to."

"I wouldn't go if I didn't have to." He pulled me close and caught my chin with two strong fingers. "We aren't going backwards," he said. "Promise me we won't go backwards."

I smoothed my hands down his chest, feeling the roll and flex of his muscles under my touch. "Okay."

His fingers tightened at my waist. "Say it."

I spread my hands up his shoulders and around his neck, letting my fingers curl in the soft strands of his hair. "We aren't going backwards," I said.

Eyes shining, he bowed his head to mine and kissed me softly. "So, you aren't going to hide from me at Blanchard's anymore?"

I froze in his arms. "What?"

His soft laugh rumbled between us. "Never mind."

I let my eyes flutter shut as his hands roamed over my hips. His touch felt so good I didn't want it to stop. It was a good thing he had to go because I might not be able to restrain myself from doing something very embarrassing like begging if he kept touching me.

Giving him a little push, I put some space between us. "You're gonna be late," I said.

He sighed heavily and released me. "Summer's with her dad this weekend, right?"

"Yes." My brows pulled together, worry rearing its ugly head again. "I hope he didn't ditch her off on a sitter."

Thatcher didn't say anything, just watched me with a steady gaze.

"I get a little anxious when she's with him," I admitted. "He doesn't have the best track record."

"I get it," Thatcher said. "Your worries don't have to disappear, but you can put them in the back seat for a bit and let yourself take the wheel."

I blinked up at him, a smile curving my lips. "How did you get smart?"

He grinned and snagged my wrist, pulling me close again. "Years of therapy." His arm cinched around my waist. "So, you're mine later."

Heat exploded in my chest. "Okay."

He lifted my hand and wrapped it around his neck. "Kiss me again."

My belly quivered. "You're kind of bossy."

His face lowered to hover above mine. "You like it."

I raised up onto my toes and kissed him, putting my entire body into it, because he was right. I liked it a whole lot.

Seventeen

A sinking feeling hit my gut as I rang Pressly's doorbell for the third time. Pulling out my phone, I checked the time.

Yep, three o'clock. I was on time to the minute. Leftover habit from my military days.

Scrolling to Pressly's number, I hit Call. Every muscle in my body tensed while the phone rang. It had only been a few hours since she'd promised me we wouldn't go backward. And here she was avoiding me again.

What ringtone had she assigned to me? Hopefully, it was better than "The Twilight Zone."

When she answered with a breathless greeting, my shoulders relaxed.

"Are you trying to ditch me?" I asked.

"No," she said. "Why?"

The tension in my body went down another notch. "I thought you were trying to avoid me again."

"What? Where are you?"

I heard Aslan's barks both on the other side of the door and through the phone. "I'm standing on your porch, ringing your doorbell."

"Try it again," she said with a heavy sigh. "It must be broken."

I pressed the doorbell a few times, listening for the chime inside the house. Nothing happened.

"Are you ringing it?" she asked.

"Yes." I held my finger down on the button. "I'm ringing it."

"You've got to be kidding me." She sounded breathless, as if she was running down the stairs. "I'll have to add it to the list."

Footsteps sounded on the other side of the door, and a moment later, it flew open. Pressly stood there with flushed cheeks and bright eyes, her phone pressed to her ear.

"Damn." My gaze dropped from her face down her fitted red sweater and slim jeans. She looked hot as hell. "Red is definitely your color," I said. "You look amazing."

Her cheeks brightened to match her sweater, and she smoothed her hands down her denim-clad thighs. "I wasn't sure if this was okay."

She could have worn a paper bag and rubber boots and looked sexy. "More than okay."

I offered her the bouquet of flowers in my hand, and her smile beamed. "You brought me tulips!"

Warmth spread through me at her obvious delight. "You like them?"

"They're my favorite flower."

I made a mental note to plant tulips when I finally got to landscaping.

She turned to go into her house, and my gaze dropped to her ass. Holy shit. I had a full afternoon of activities planned for our first date, but one look at her fine ass in those jeans made me want to spend the day in bed with her. Exploring every inch of her.

"I'll just put these in some water."

I waited at the door, distracting myself from dirty thoughts by petting Aslan. He'd come a long way since Pressly had adopted him. Lacey had told me the sob story of Aslan being returned to the shelter multiple times because of his bad behavior. She'd even tried to get me to take him, but Pressly had rescued him before I'd gotten the chance.

"You're not such a bad guy, are you?" I scratched him behind the ears.

His back leg thumped the floor, and his tail wagged.

"Okay," Pressly said, appearing at the door with her purse over her shoulder. "I'm ready. You think this is okay? I wasn't sure what you meant about getting dirty." Her blue eyes looked innocent, but the sly smile on her lips went straight to my dick.

If I didn't get her out of her house and soon, we wouldn't be leaving.

I grabbed her hand and pulled her over the threshold. "You're perfect," I said, glancing down at her designer boots. "I don't know about the shoes, though."

"They're the oldest pair I have," she said, closing the door behind her. "You never said what we were doing."

We walked across the lawn to my Jeep. "You'll see."

She frowned, and a cute little dent appeared between her brows. "I don't like surprises."

I leaned over and opened the passenger door for her. "I thought everyone liked surprises."

"Not me."

"Duly noted," I said. I filed that bit of information away next to her favorite flower in all things Pressly Vinroot.

She paused and turned to me, her eyes bluer than the Carolina sky. "Are you gonna tell me or not?"

She was so close I could smell the subtle scent of her perfume.

Elegant and expensive, Pressly was so out of my league. But that had never stopped me from wanting her.

Every fiber of my being wanted her.

Brushing a strand of hair off her face, I caressed her cheek with a sweep of my thumb. "I'll tell you," I said, my voice a little rougher than I'd intended. "But we need to get in the car before I change my mind and drag you inside for the rest of the weekend."

She sucked in a sharp breath and then laughed softly. Arousal rippled through me at the sound.

"I was wondering if maybe I'd imagined what had happened this morning," she said.

I'd imagined kissing her a million times, but it hadn't compared to the real thing.

Cupping her cheek, I dipped my head to hers. One little kiss wouldn't hurt.

She sighed as our lips touched. A soft, feminine sound that did nothing to ease the ache to bury myself inside her.

The years melted away as our mouths came together. I felt eighteen again, as if my life hadn't unfolded yet. Everything was ripe and mine for the taking.

I brushed my tongue over the seam of her lips, and they parted eagerly. Her tongue licked into my mouth, and a low growl of need rumbled in my chest.

Curling my hand around her neck, I angled my head to kiss her deeper. Our tongues stroked together, and an electric current raced through me. The shock made me conscious of how much more I wanted from her.

I wanted her body and soul. All of her. The tulips and the surprises.

I broke the kiss and dragged in a breath. Our eyes locked, and only one word filled my mind when I looked at her—mine. She was mine.

Her cheeks flushed, and she stared at my mouth. "We're giving the neighbors a show."

I glanced over my shoulder and saw Chelsea Taylor, the gossip queen of our neighborhood, strolling by with her poodle mix. "Fuck the neighbors."

Pressly laughed, and her hands fluttered up to my chest as if she couldn't resist touching me. "Maybe just one of the neighbors."

I forced myself to take a step back before I grabbed her and carried her inside.

"Later," I said.

A warm blush spread over her cheeks as I closed the passenger door and jogged around the front of the Jeep. Chelsea Taylor was still staring in our direction, and I raised a hand in greeting.

"Hello, Chelsea!"

She waved back, her face bright with curiosity. "Hello, Thatcher."

Now the whole neighborhood would know about me and Pressly. Good. They might as well get used to it.

"So, where are we going?" Pressly asked as I settled behind the wheel.

She turned to face me, and I was hit with another wave of appreciation for her stunning beauty. She had large, expressive eyes framed by thick lashes, high cheekbones, and full lips. It took all my willpower not to lean forward and kiss her pretty mouth.

I put the Jeep in reverse and rested my hand on the back of her seat as I turned to look out the back window. "Have you ever been to the Loch Norman Lumberjack Festival?"

Pressly clapped her hands together in excitement. "Of course! My dad used to take us every year. Beckett even won the stone throw event for kids one year."

"Of course he did." I wouldn't put it past Beckett to win anything he put his mind to. That summer I'd coached him at baseball, he hadn't been the best athlete, but he'd been the smartest. "Did you ever compete?"

Pressly snickered. "God, no."

"Aw, come on. You'd make the cutest lumberjill. I wouldn't mind watching you in the pole climb."

She laughed harder, and I loved the sound of it.

"Or maybe the tree felling competition."

"I'd probably chop off a limb."

I reached for her hand and linked our fingers. "Better not compete," I said. "I like you with all your limbs attached."

We drove to the outskirts of town, chatting lightly about the events and Pressly's memories of the festival.

Her earlier worries about Summer spending the weekend with her father had been pushed aside, and her face glowed with excitement. "Have you tried haggis?" she asked.

"No."

"You have to try it. It's horrible," she said with a grimace. "And Scotch eggs, too."

"I'll have to take a rain check on both of those," I said. "I'm on a strict diet for the next few weeks."

"Diet?" She scoffed. "Why? You don't have an ounce of fat on you."

"Leaner and stronger is a good strategy for the fight," I said. "But it means I have to give up deep-fried sausage-covered eggs." And pizza. And beer.

Pressly crossed her legs and focused her attention on the scenery. "So, you're really going through with the fight?"

"You're not worried about me, are you?"

Her blue gaze shot to me. "I remember doctoring you up after you got in a fight," she said. "It wasn't fun seeing you like that."

I took her hand and squeezed her fingers. "I appreciate your concern, but I'm not a kid anymore. I've been boxing for years. I know what I'm doing."

She sighed heavily. "I hate violence."

I chuckled. "It's sport, not violence." I brushed a kiss over her knuckles, then placed her hand on my thigh so I could use both hands to steer the Jeep into the gravel lot at the event. "Don't worry about me, okay?"

"I can't help worrying about people I care about," she said.

Something shifted and swelled inside me with her admission. I parked the Jeep between two oversized trucks and leaned forward to kiss her again.

"I care about you, too," I said.

The truth was I never stopped.

Eighteen

We couldn't seem to stop touching. His arm wrapped around my waist, my head leaned against his shoulder, and our hands sought each other's. Fingers clasped, we strolled through the festival, stopping to watch the events.

Thatcher knew half the people there and didn't mind stopping to have a chat. He was patient and kind, introducing me whenever possible and holding my hand the whole time.

"People are going to think I'm your girlfriend," I said.

He shrugged. "I don't care what people think. Do you?"

I had my daughter to think of and my job as manager at the hotel. But this was Thatcher. He was worth the gossip, and Summer loved him.

"It's risky," I said. "This is our first date—how do you even know if you like me?"

He wrapped his arm around my shoulders, tucking me against his side. "This is not our first date," he said.

"It's our first date as adults," I said. "It's different."

He gripped my shoulder tightly and dropped his head to nuzzle my hair. "You make me feel like a kid again."

He plied me with warm apple cider and fish and chips. We

watched the bagpipes, placed a friendly bet on the log-felling relay contest, and teamed up to win a game of tug-of-war against a gaggle of teenagers.

I basked in all the small-town goodness I'd missed about Mossy Oak.

Thatcher stopped in front of a vintage portrait studio made to look like a frontier cabin and quirked a brow at me. "What do you think? Should we document our official first date?"

The log cabin backdrop featured an old washtub and a bearskin rug. A selection of costumes hung from a rack. "Sure," I said. "But you have to let me pick what you wear."

His lips curved in a smile. "Deal."

I flipped through the clothes on the rack, laughing harder with each one. There was a kilt, a red thermal onesie, and a padded sleeveless jacket with a beanie.

My eagerness to see Thatcher in flannel again won out, and I grabbed the vest and beanie.

"Here you go," I said, handing him the clothes I'd selected. "The jeans you're wearing are fine." The way his jeans hugged his strong thighs and perfect ass was more than fine, but I kept that to myself.

Eyes twinkling, he handed me his selection. "You can keep your boots on."

"Where's the rest of it?" I asked, looking at the skimpy outfit.

He pushed the costume into my chest and steered me in the direction of the women's changing room. "I'll see you in a few minutes."

"Thatcher," I said, holding the costume at arm's length. "I *cannot* wear this."

The corner of his lip lifted. "Are you backing out?"

I grimaced. "No."

"Then I'll see you in a minute." He grinned and ducked into the men's changing room.

With great reluctance, I changed into the denim overall shorts and cropped top. The shorts were made with a healthy dose of Lycra that made them one-size-fits-snug. They barely covered my ass, and the plaid tie-front cropped top was even worse.

A knock at the door sounded, and I jumped.

"Pressly?" Thatcher called. "Are you ready?"

I stared at myself in the mirror. All that flesh was too much. I couldn't do it. Clearing my throat, I went to the door and leaned against it. "I can't wear this," I said. "You have to pick something else."

The doorknob rattled. "Open the door, babe," he said in a husky command.

I unlocked the door and stepped back, allowing Thatcher into the small space. Arms crossed over my bare midriff, I stood before him in my sexy lumberjill glory. "Satisfied?" I asked, hooking my thumbs in the suspenders.

He pushed the door closed behind him and leaned against it. His gaze roamed over me like a blaze of heat.

"Holy shit," he murmured, shaking his head. "You are so fucking hot."

Electricity buzzed through me, but my eyes were fixed on him. He was wearing the red flannel coat, opened to reveal his bare chest. His well-defined pecs and washboard stomach were much better in real life than they were in the calendar photo.

"Turn around," he said, his voice a husky growl.

"What?" My gaze flickered up to his face, and I saw the hungry look in his eyes.

"Turn around. I want to see your ass in those shorts."

My heart jumped to my throat, and I put one foot forward, spinning on my heel.

"Fuck," he groaned. "You can not go out there like that."

I turned around to look at myself in the mirror. My breasts spilled out of the cropped top, and the shorts barely covered my thighs. "I told you."

He stepped up behind me, and our gazes locked in the mirror.

An electric charge zinged between us. I could feel the crackle in the air and hear the sound of his breath.

His hand came to rest lightly at my hip, then trailed slowly up my side. His soft touch made my belly tighten, and his hot blue gaze made me feel naked.

Tracing a path just under my breasts, he reached for the knot tied in the top and tugged. The top fell open, and my breasts spilled out. I gasped as he pushed the fabric away and filled both his hands with my soft flesh.

His front pressed to my back, and I felt the hard length of his erection pressing into my ass. Caressing my breasts, he bent to kiss the crook of my neck where it met my shoulder.

A moan escaped my mouth as his teeth nipped my neck while his hands continued to massage my breasts and rub my nipples into stiff peaks.

Opening my eyes, I saw he was watching us, his eyes fixed on my flushed chest. I'd never seen anything sexier than the way he was looking at me. At us.

We fit perfectly together. His chin rested on top of my head, and when I leaned against his solid chest, I felt like nothing could harm me ever again.

One of his hands slid up to cup my chin, turning my face up and back to receive his kiss. His mouth was hot and hungry on mine, his arm locking me into place against his solid chest.

My bones went liquid as I leaned against him, rubbing my ass against the hard bulge in his jeans. His strong fingers held my face as he kissed me hard, stealing my breath. His tongue darted into my mouth, teasing and tasting in hot little licks.

He pinched my nipple. The feel of his rough fingers against my sensitive flesh made me arch against him for more and moan his name.

Groaning in response, he pushed his thick cock against my ass, and I almost lost my mind. I reached back to rub the outline of his cock in his jeans, and he sucked in a sharp breath.

"Fucking hell," he rasped. "Feel what you do to me?" He

rocked against me, pinning my eyes in the mirror as his hand trailed down my waist. "What do I do to you?"

His fingers slid under the waistband of my shorts and kept going. He pushed aside my panties and felt how wet I was for him.

My entire body throbbed for his touch as he slid one finger down my slick seam and circled back to my clit.

"So wet for me." His voice was thick with need as he stroked me.

I ran my hand up and over the length of him, feeling the throb of his cock through the denim of his jeans.

His arm came around me, and he squeezed my breast, pinching my nipple as the fingers of his other hand played over my clit.

My body tightened and pulsed, and I felt the orgasm building. The door was unlocked, and anyone could walk in at any moment, which should have worried me, but it only added to my excitement.

"Mmm," he moaned against my neck, scraping the rough sandpaper of his beard along my skin. "That's it. You are so fucking hot, baby."

I ground my hips against him, moaning shamelessly as the pleasure built inside me. I reached for his zipper, wanting to feel the hot brand of his shaft in my hand or, better yet, buried inside me, but he shifted away.

"Open your eyes. Look at yourself."

His voice was a low, lusty growl that shot through every cell in my body.

I opened my eyes and saw myself in the mirror. Only it wasn't someone I recognized. The woman with the tumble of hair covering her bare breasts locked in the strong embrace of her lover wasn't someone I knew.

Flush-stained cheeks and swollen lips, eyes shining like hot lava—the woman in the mirror was a sex goddess.

His eyes devoured me with a raw, hungry look that made me feel like the woman in the mirror.

Blood roared through my body. Every pulse of my heart sent a surge of arousal racing through me.

My knees went weak, and Thatcher held me up. His arms were strong, his body solid. Stroking his fingers inside me, slipping through the wetness, he knew instinctively how to touch me.

His gaze lifted to mine, and the tender look he gave me tore down the walls I'd erected around my heart. He locked his arms around me, his fingers playing over my body in just the right rhythm.

He kissed my neck, his voice a low rumble at my ear. "Come for me."

His dirty words unleashed an explosion inside me, and I came. For him. For me. For that girl I used to be.

I came and kept coming as he stroked his fingers inside me. Waves of pleasure consumed me, and I came hard to make up for all the years it had been since a man made me feel safe enough to be wild.

Nineteen

Silence filled the car, tension throbbing thick and heavy between us as I pulled up to my house and cut the engine. The street was dark, our neighbors safely tucked in for the night, but Pressly and I weren't nearly done.

Something had changed in her when we'd left the dressing room. We'd sat for the portrait—her in the sexy shorts and cropped top that pushed her breasts up to her neck, me in the ridiculous plaid coat with no sleeves or buttons. We'd smiled for the camera and joked about how silly we looked and what the hell we were going to do with the portrait, but our laughs had been forced, our minds on what was coming next.

We'd crossed a line in that dressing room. When I'd touched her, making her come in long hot pulses against my hand, we'd jumped out of the frying pan into the fire.

There was no going back to the friend zone now.

She'd barely said a word on the drive home, and I worried I'd pushed too far too fast.

I swear, I hadn't meant to touch her. But seeing her in that skimpy outfit that I'd picked out, knowing how fucking hot she would look in it, made my dick take over my brain.

And when she'd melted against me, her hips rocking against my hard cock, her gaze wild and carefree, I'd lost my control.

There was no taking it slow, building trust, or breaking down her walls. There was only touching her, pleasing her, making her come.

"Thatcher?" Her voice caught a little as she turned to face me. Shadows danced across her face, and she couldn't quite meet my eyes.

I swallowed roughly, prepping my ego to take the hit when she let me down. Not that I was gonna accept it.

Hell no.

Not after what had happened in that changing room.

I wasn't about to give up on us. I wouldn't turn around, but if she wanted me to take my foot off the gas, I could handle that.

"Yeah?" I asked, my voice a gruff bark slicing through the tension.

She put her hand on my thigh and leaned across the seat. "Your place or mine?"

My breath released on a low chuckle, and I let my head fall back as her hand moved higher, fingers skimming the outline of my stiffening cock. "I don't care, babe," I said.

She leaned closer, her soft hair a tickle on my cheek, her hand rising higher to fully cup and flatten against me. "If you come to mine, you can stay all night."

Pleasure fired down my spine, and I let out a low moan. "I like that option."

She sifted her fingers through my hair, moving it off my neck so she could press her lips below my jaw. "Or I could take care of you right now," she said, teeth grazing over my earlobe. Her breath was warm in my ear, her tongue a slick caress. "Pay you back." She bit down gently on my earlobe as her fingers worked open the button of my jeans.

Pleasure fired through me, but I reached down to circle her wrist before she could snag my zipper down. "Tempting. But I'd rather have you in a bed."

She pulled back, her eyes flicking over me with sly humor. "You're getting old, Thatcher."

I laughed and cinched my arms around her waist. With one strong pull, she was sprawled across my lap, the soft curves of her ass pressing into everywhere I was hard. I closed my mouth over hers, kissing her deeply.

She tasted like the apple cider we'd drank and smelled of her expensive perfume. I molded my hands to her back, pulling her closer, thrusting my tongue deeper until I was drunk on her.

Wiggling closer, she straddled my lap and rocked her hips against mine. I gripped her ass and hoisted her higher.

"There's nothing wrong with getting old," I said. Pushing open the door, I shifted and slid my feet to the ground. "We don't have to do it in my Jeep like teenagers." I set her on the driveway, my hands still clutching her ass. "I need to check on Daisy, then I want you in a bed. Naked. I don't care whose."

She smiled up at me, a sexy gleam in her eyes. "My house," she said. Reaching into the Jeep to grab her purse, she slid by me. "Bring Daisy if you want to." She tossed a sassy grin over her shoulder. "And condoms."

I watched her walk to her door, my eyes glued to her heart-shaped ass. Pressure swelled uncomfortably inside me. My heart, my chest, my dick—everywhere. I pulsed with need for her.

As her door closed, I snapped out of my trance and hurried to my door.

I couldn't fuck this up with her. I couldn't lose her again.

Daisy waited at the door for me, her tail thumping the floor in welcome. I let her out the back, then took the stairs two at a time up to my bathroom, where I found a box of condoms. I grabbed a few, then, better safe than sorry, grabbed a few more.

Knocking on her door, I tried to act casual, but the moment she opened it, I couldn't get my hands on her fast enough.

She let out a little squeak of surprise as I pulled her into my arms and kissed her. The sound became a moan as our tongues slid together, picking up right where they'd left off.

Her hands roamed over my chest, across my shoulders, down my back. Stealing under my shirt, her palms spread up the back of my waist.

"Off," she said, breaking the kiss long enough to pull back, yanking at the hem of my shirt.

I released her long enough to pull my shirt over my head and drop it to the floor.

When I reached for her again, she took a step back, holding up her hands. "Whoa." Her eyes darkened and roamed over me hungrily. "I might need a minute."

I laughed and took a step forward, but she shook her head, biting her lip. "Do you want to take a picture?" I asked, only half teasing.

Her gaze flashed up to mine. "Maybe later."

"Come here." I grabbed her around the waist, hauling her close. I kissed her hard, then reached down and hoisted her up so her legs wrapped around my hips.

Her laugh vibrated between us. "You don't have to carry me. I promise I won't run away."

Her words had been playful, but I felt them deep. Something clicked inside my chest, and I set her down on the floor, cupping her face in my hands. "Say that again," I said.

She met my gaze with an unblinking stare. "I'm not going anywhere," she said.

I lowered my lips to hers. We kissed, tenderly and unhurried. I slowly backed her up a few steps, then slid my hands under her sweater and pushed it up her chest. She lifted her arms, and I pulled it off, letting it drop before seeking out the button of her jeans.

She reached down and unzipped her boots, kicking them off before running her hands up my chest in a slow exploration.

"It's not fair you look like that," she said, pouting a little as she dragged her gaze up my chest.

I bent and unlaced my boots, dropping them next to hers at the living room entrance. She was wearing a satin bra identical to the one Daisy had stolen on move-in day, and the creamy tops of her breasts pushed over the cups in a way my imagination hadn't done justice.

I licked my lips. This was going to be a long night because I was going to drag out every fucking second of it.

Pulling her back into my arms, I kissed her and backed her into the living room. We moved together, unable to stop touching and kissing long enough to look where we were going.

We bumped into the arm of the sofa, nearly going down.

"You okay?" I panted.

"I'm good," she said, clutching my shoulders.

I undid her bra and slid it off her shoulders. "Still good?" I asked, holding her gaze even though I was dying to look down. I was probably checking in too much, but I couldn't fuck this up and scare her off.

Smiling a little, she tossed her bra to the floor. "You can look at me," she said. "I like the way you look at me."

My gaze dropped to her chest, taking in her flushed breasts, the nip of her waist, and the generous flare of her hips. God, how did I get so lucky?

Undoing her jeans, I pushed them down, hooking her thong as I went. "They don't match," I said absently.

"What?" Her voice was thick with lust.

"I thought you'd be the matching-set kind of woman," I said.

She leaned back on the arm of the sofa, allowing me to slide her jeans and panties down her legs and over her feet. "Disappointed?"

I grabbed her hand and placed it on the thick bulge in my jeans. "Do I feel disappointed?"

She dragged me down to kiss her, moving her hand up and down my hard length over my jeans in rough strokes. The friction made me want to explode, and just when I couldn't take it anymore, she worked my button open and pulled the zipper down.

Yanking back, she met my gaze. "You're not wearing underwear," she said.

I took advantage of her open mouth and kissed her deeply. "Never wear them."

"Jesus," she said, fisting my hard cock as it sprang free in her hand. "You've been running around Mossy Oak with no underwear on all this time?"

I pulled in a sharp breath as her slim fingers encircled me and gave my length a long, exploring stroke. She shoved my jeans down my hips but not before I managed to grab a condom from the back pocket.

Ripping it open, I rolled it down over my throbbing cock and bent her back on the sofa.

We didn't make it to the bedroom, but as I sank into her, I felt like I'd come home.

We moved together, slow and intense, then fast and wild. I started out on top but somehow ended up under her as she straddled my thighs and took control.

It was a fantasy come true watching her ride me. Her back arched, and her breasts bounced, so close I couldn't help reaching up to suck one rosy nipple into my mouth. When I swirled my tongue over her hard flesh, she cried out, her entire body going tense.

I felt the orgasm cascade over her. Her pussy fluttered, clenching my cock in her tight sheath, and that was it for me.

I'd hoped to last longer, but I couldn't hold back when she pinned me to the sofa and rocked against me, her slick heat so tight and hot. I grabbed her hips and drove deep, surrendering to the release pounding through me.

She collapsed against me, and I held her close, regretting I hadn't lasted nearly as long as I'd intended.

Brightening, I realized that was only round one. We had all night together.

Twenty

Heaven. I'd died and gone to heaven. I was out of breath and sweaty, but I hadn't felt so good in years. Maybe ever.

I'd been making do with my battery-operated friend, but it was being retired in favor of the man next door.

His hands tightened around my waist, and he plucked me off his chest. "Be right back," he said, sliding out from under me to stride into the kitchen and take care of the condom.

I watched his ass, enjoying the view from the back and then the front as he came back a moment later. He looked sexy as hell stalking naked through my living room.

Grabbing his jeans, he shook another condom from his pocket and reached down to haul me to my feet. "Bedroom," he growled. "Now."

I wrapped my arms around his neck, letting him support my weight when my legs went boneless. He cinched me to his chest and guided me backward.

When I'd rolled out of my bed that morning, I'd never pictured my day to end like this. It had been years since I'd had an orgasm, and now I'd had two in one night. From the way Thatcher was kissing me and the hard press of his cock against my thigh, I didn't think it was a stretch to imagine another orgasm in the cards.

"I Will Always Love You" by Whitney Houston filled the air, and I pulled back from Thatcher's embrace. "That's Summer," I said, instantly feeling the mom guilt sink in.

I hadn't thought about my daughter for hours. Plus, I was naked and had just had sex on our brand-new sofa.

It wasn't my proudest mom moment. I hurried across the room and grabbed my phone from my purse.

"Hello?" I said, a little breathless.

"Mom!" Summer cried. "Guess what?"

My shoulders relaxed. From the sound of her excited voice, everything was okay. I met Thatcher's concerned gaze and smiled.

"What?" I asked Summer, stooping to grab our discarded clothes from the floor.

"Dad is taking me to see a music festival tomorrow. It's gonna be awesome!"

"Oh?" I raised my gaze to Thatcher, who was waiting for me at the bottom of the stairs. I crossed the room and took his hand, letting him lead me up the stairs to my bedroom as Summer told me the plans for the next day with her dad.

It was hard not to be jealous, but I reminded myself that Summer deserved to have fun with her dad. "That's great, sweetie."

"He said he's gonna teach me to fly someday," she said. "So I can fly his jet."

I repressed a sigh. "That's nice, but you'll probably have to get your driver's license first."

"So, it's okay if I go to Charleston for the festival? Dad said I had to ask you."

Fucking Jeff. I wanted to strangle him half the time.

"Do you need to talk to him?" Summer asked.

"No," I barked. Talking to Jeff was the last thing I wanted to do. "It's fine. I will see you tomorrow night."

Thatcher pulled me into the bedroom. I dropped my clothes

and clutched his shoulder. His skin was flawless and smooth, unmarked except for the small tattoo on the back of his shoulder. I rose up to my toes to inspect it, and he swatted me away.

"Dad says he wants to talk to you," Summer said.

My stomach clenched. "Put him on."

"Hey, Pressly."

"Jeff."

Thatcher ran his hand up my side, letting his fingers brush the side of my breast. He guided me to the bed and pushed me down on the mattress.

"You haven't been answering my calls," Jeff said.

"Just text me," I said, breathing hard as Thatcher placed the remaining condoms on the nightstand.

"I wanted to make sure you were okay with everything this weekend."

"As long as you keep her safe and return her on time, you and Summer can do what you want."

Jeff's voice dropped. "Are you with him now?"

I pulled in a deep breath and looked up at Thatcher. He stood naked at the edge of the bed, his cock hard and proud between his legs, his muscled torso glowing in the soft lamplight. He raised a brow and nudged my legs apart, coming to stand between them.

"Goodbye, Jeff. See you tomorrow night." I swiped to hang up and tossed my phone on the bed.

Smiling up at Thatcher, I scooted back and reached for the lamp. He grabbed my wrist and stopped me.

"No." His voice was a firm command. "The light stays on."

A flush spread up my chest, but who was I to argue when I had such a magnificent man to look at? I reached up to touch his chest, running my fingers across the fine dusting of hair on his pecs.

"What's that tattoo?" I asked, peering up at his shoulder. "Is it Tweety Bird?"

He nodded solemnly. "Army tattoo," he said. "I got it right after boot camp."

"It's cute," I said, giving it a kiss.

He smiled and pushed me back onto the mattress, then covered me with his solid weight.

His mouth sank onto mine, and we kissed long and deep. The frenzied hunger we'd had in the living room was gone, replaced by something sweet and tender. His lips explored my mouth, then trailed down my chin to my neck. He kissed my breasts, lavishing my nipples with his tongue and teeth before moving back to take my mouth again.

We took our time, kissing and touching until I begged him to fill me.

When he finally rolled the condom over his thick erection, I was wetter than I'd ever been. He dragged the head of his covered cock along my slick seam.

It felt so good I trembled.

"I love how you respond to me," he said, bracing his elbows on either side of my head.

He leaned down to take my mouth, the soft strands of his hair caressing my cheeks. Slowly, he sank inside me, and we moved together, riding the waves of pleasure.

"You feel so good," I said, skimming my fingers down the tight muscles of his back.

He thrust into me, deeper with every stroke. I felt the orgasm building like a rumbling wave, and I squeezed my eyes shut, allowing it to wash over me.

"Look at me," Thatcher said, his voice a stern command I was growing more used to obeying.

I opened my eyes and met his bright blue gaze. Desire surged between us, sizzling like lightning.

He pounded into me, each thrust harder and deeper. The sound of our bodies coming together with little moans and sighs filled the room. Sweat beaded on my hairline as heat and friction slicked our bodies.

"I wanted this since the first time I saw you at Blanchard's," he said, reaching down to side his fingers between us. "I wanted to see you come on my cock." He drove into me. "On my fingers." His heavy cock dragged in and out of me. "On my fucking face."

The sound of his voice, thick and hoarse with desire, drove me over the edge, and I cried out as the orgasm ripped through me.

He stiffened and thrust into me again, groaning as he emptied his release. His mouth came down on mine, sealing everything we'd done with a rough kiss.

Still breathing hard, he rolled off me and went to take care of the condom.

I hadn't had sex in years, and I'd just done it twice in one night. This was going to be hard to top.

I heard the sound of running water, and a moment later Thatcher, came back into the bedroom and grabbed my hand. "Your bathtub is big enough for two," he said.

"I know."

He tugged me into his arms and steered me toward the bathroom. "Let's try it out."

I sighed in disappointment. "The jets don't work."

"I can take a look at that for you," he said, laughing when my mouth dropped. "Maybe later."

He lowered himself into the tub and scooted back to make room for me. I secured my hair on top of my head and joined him, sighing as I sank into the warm water.

"Come here," he said, opening his arms.

I rested with my back against his front, and he picked up the soap. Slowly circling it over my body, he massaged me into a relaxed state of bliss.

"Can I ask you something?"

I stiffened a little. "Sure."

"What made you buy this place?"

I relaxed and tipped my chin back to look at him. "I've loved this place for years."

"Really? I thought you were more the modern high-rise type."

"I can't explain," I said. "I've just always been in love with it. I used to drive out of my way just to pass it." I reached up to tuck a strand of his dark blond hair that hung over his cheek. "The yard was always beautifully manicured, and there was the sweetest tire swing hanging from the gigantic maple. I imagined what the family inside was like. In my mind, they were perfect."

"No one is perfect."

"I know that."

He was quiet for so long I thought he'd fallen asleep. Then his mouth moved over my ear in a soft caress.

"I'm crazy about you," he said. "I have been forever. You were that girl that got away."

And he was that guy.

This was all moving very fast, and suddenly, I realized what we'd done. This wasn't just about sex or scratching an itch. There was something special between us. There always had been.

"I've got baggage," I said.

He laughed, pulling my back tighter to his front. "Me too."

"I'm divorced," I said. I never thought I'd say those words.

"He didn't deserve you."

I tipped my head back and kissed him. "Thank you."

The kiss deepened, and before I knew it, he was lifting me out of the tub and carrying me back to the bed.

March 2002

Dear Pressly,

I think I fucked up. This isn't fixing anything. After my dad died, I thought it was the right thing to do, but what am I doing in the middle of nowhere on a mission no one even knows about?

They say we are here to keep the peace, but there hasn't been peace here for so long, no one even knows what the word means anymore.

I can't trust any of the locals. It's hard to tell what side they're on. We made friends with some of the students, thinking a kind word would help their rehabilitation into society, but then they stole our weapons and attacked each other.

Four kids died, but the saddest part was the

way the others fed on the violence. It's been in them for too long.

This country is so rich, but it has been robbed and ravaged for too long. It can never be whole again.

Word is we are getting out of here soon and heading to Freetown. I will write from there.

I hope you are well and enjoying your last year of high school before the real world starts.

I think about you every day.

I love you.

Sincerely, Thatcher Hayes

Twenty-One

My phone chimed from the pocket of my jeans at the foot of the bed.

Fuck.

It couldn't be four o'clock yet. I'd only just closed my eyes.

I untangled myself from Pressly and fished my phone from my pocket. Four a.m. had never felt so early.

I shut off my alarm, moving quietly so I didn't wake her. We'd been up half the night, and she needed her sleep.

She looked like a goddess lying naked on the bed. All sexy curves, flowing hair, and creamy skin. She was a fantasy come true.

We'd gone at least five rounds last night, but I still wanted her. If I didn't have to meet Jay for a run before training, I would have climbed back in bed with her.

I padded over to the bed and tucked the sheet around her. She smelled like lavender soap and sex, and the little sigh she made had my cock rising with anticipation.

Down, boy. I had to run. Literally. Plus, we were out of condoms.

Pressly stirred and opened her eyes, blinking slowly up at me. "What time is it?"

"Too early," I said. "Go back to sleep."

Shifting to prop herself on one elbow, she trailed her fingers down my chest. "How do you expect me to go back to sleep when you look like that?"

I dragged in a breath as her touch ignited a flame inside me. Her hand dipped lower, and my cock rose obligingly.

"Good morning," she said to my lower half, fingers encircling me.

Our eyes locked in the dimly lit room, and the only sound was our heavy breaths. A naughty gleam came into her eyes as she stroked me.

My lips curved, and I tugged the sheet down and cupped her breast, plucking her nipple into a hard peak.

She made another noise, and I pushed her down on the bed, covering her mouth with mine.

Fuck a five-mile run. There were better ways to get cardio.

She arched against me, and the tip of my cock slicked through her wetness.

"We used all the condoms," I said.

She tucked my hair behind my ear, cupping my face. "I want you."

I glanced down between us where we were lined up perfectly. My cock glistened with her wetness, straining between us. "I want you, too."

She reached down and guided me inside her, and we both let out a low moan as I sank deep. It felt unbelievable to be so close to her, skin to skin with no barriers.

"You're so fucking sexy." I pulled out all the way and rubbed the tip of my cock over her swollen clit before sliding inside her again.

Her eyes flashed open, hot with arousal. "You feel so good. I didn't know it could feel like this." She smiled wickedly. "I'm going to want this all the time."

A grin tugged at my mouth. "I'm going to give this to you all the time."

She clutched my shoulders, arching against me, holding on as I fucked her hard enough to make the headboard bang the wall.

I grabbed her by the waist and dragged her down onto my cock over and over. Her breasts bouncing with every thrust was one of the sexiest things I'd ever seen.

A flush crept up her chest to stain her neck, and I knew she was close.

"Don't stop." Her fingers dug into my back. "Don't stop." The words became a chant and then a cry as the orgasm crashed over her.

Her pussy fluttered and pulsed, and I knew I couldn't hold off much longer. My blood roared, and I thrust deep one more time, pulling out before I finished inside her.

Release pulsed through me, and I came in hot spurts on the curve of her belly. She propped up on her elbows and watched with hooded eyes as I pumped my cock into my fist, a satisfied smile curving her lips.

I collapsed on the bed beside her, my chest heaving as I panted for breath. She shifted closer, her hand reaching for mine. Our fingers linked, and I let my eyes shut for a moment, basking in post orgasm bliss.

* * *

A persistent chime sounded, slowly breaking into the fantastic dream I was having.

"Thatcher." Pressly's voice sounded low and throaty near my ear.

I tightened my arm around her and rubbed my chin over her jaw. "Yeah?"

"Your phone is ringing," she said.

"Shit." I rolled off the bed and grabbed my phone from my jeans. Jay's name scrolled across the screen. I swiped to answer, at the same time pulling on my jeans. "Hello?"

"Where the fuck are you?" Jay growled.

"I'll be right down."

"I'm standing at your door, man," Jay said. "You're not here."

"I said I'll be right there."

He hung up without responding, and I shoved my phone into my pocket.

"He sounded angry," Pressly said, looking concerned.

"That's just Jay," I said. "He's an asshole." I pulled on my shirt and dropped onto the mattress. "What are you doing later?"

"I've got to work, and then I'm picking Summer up from the airport at seven."

And I had hours of training, followed by an afternoon at the store.

It looked like our fun weekend was over. But I didn't want it to end. "How about I bring over dinner?"

Pressly avoided my gaze, suddenly shy. It was a surprise, considering everything we'd done the night before and this morning. She still had my cum on her belly, but she couldn't look at me.

I tipped her chin up to meet my gaze. "I'll be here at eight."

She nodded. "Okay."

I lowered my mouth to hers for one last kiss, keeping it brief because she was too tempting, and Jay was probably going to add a mile to my run for every minute I kept him waiting.

I was early. Jeff was late.

It was the story of our lives. I'd always put in just a little extra, allowing him to enjoy slacking.

I sat in the small airport waiting room for private planes, letting my mind drift to better things than Jeff Fucking Carleton.

At least I no longer had to fake orgasms with him. That was a huge upside of divorce.

I hadn't known there were men out there who could actually please a woman. Over and over.

Jeff and his below-average penis could go to hell for all I cared.

By the time their private plane arrived, I'd put thoughts of Thatcher and his above-average penis aside.

"I need to talk to you," he said, walking us to my car.

Summer climbed into the passenger seat and pulled her book from her backpack, ignoring us.

"Go ahead." I leaned against the door, looking up at Jeff with a neutral expression.

It was easy to see how I'd fallen for him so long ago. He was classically handsome. Tall and slim, with golden-blond hair and pale eyes, he reeked of old money and sophistication.

"I want you back," he said simply, cutting right to the chase.

A bubble of laughter burst from my mouth. "You're kidding."

He gave me a cocky grin. "I'm not."

"We're divorced." I met his eyes without flinching. "I have the paperwork to prove it."

He dipped his chin, gazing deeply into my eyes. "We have a child together."

Guilt stuck me with a sharp needle. "Leave Summer out of this," I said.

"You're so stubborn." Jeff's cool facade melted, and he ran a hand through his hair. "We could have had everything."

My jaw clenched. "We did have everything," I said. "But you wanted more."

"I was confused."

I laughed without humor. "Just like all those charges on your credit card to online dating sites weren't yours?"

His eyes narrowed. "Someone stole my identity."

I sighed and reached for my door. "I don't believe a word that comes out of your mouth."

"Don't go," Jeff said, placing his hand over mine.

My shoulders straightened, and I poked out my chin. "I left a long time ago."

Jeff averted his gaze and backed away from the car, allowing me to get in and drive away. I felt numb as I pulled out of the parking lot and started toward home.

"Did you have a good time?" I asked Summer.

She lifted her head from her book and nodded. "It was okay," she said. "I missed Aslan."

I smiled. "He missed you, too." I reached out to touch her hand. "Thatcher is coming over tonight with some dinner. Hope you're hungry."

She nodded and went back to her book. "I hope it's pizza."

At the next stoplight, I texted Thatcher to suggest pizza for dinner. He texted back almost immediately, saying he'd be over with a large pizza shortly.

"Dad's got a new girlfriend," Summer said without looking up from her book.

My heart jolted. "What?"

"She's pretty cool, I guess."

A silent scream formed in my throat, and I gripped the steering wheel tightly. He'd just been begging to have me back. The man had no boundaries. I glanced at Summer. Maybe she was mistaken.

"Did you meet her?"

"Yeah," Summer said. "She lives in Charleston. We spent the day with her."

A wave of nausea churned in my stomach. "You spent the day with her? Today?"

Summer nodded and went back to her book. I forced myself to focus on driving and not plotting Jeff's slow, painful death.

He'd always been a liar, but I hadn't realized how devious he was. He didn't care about getting back together with me; he just didn't want me to be with someone else. Having Thatcher in my life meant he'd been replaced, and Jeff couldn't stand being replaced.

We didn't say anything for the rest of the drive home, and when we pulled into the garage, I realized Summer had fallen asleep.

Her book sat limply in her lap, and her chin rested on her chest. She was breathing deeply, her face angelic in sleep.

Hot tears formed behind my eyes, and emotions swelled inside me. Love. Guilt. Regret. Tenderness.

I watched her sleep for a long moment before reaching over to gently nudge her. She was so tired she didn't even stir. I smiled fondly, remembering how I'd driven her around in the car when she couldn't fall asleep as a baby. I'd carried her in her car seat back into the house, afraid to move her in case she woke up.

She was too big for me to carry now, but she'd always be my

baby girl, the best thing Jeff and I had ever done together.

Tears slid down my cheeks as waves of emotions crashed over me. A sob stuck in my throat, and my chest constricted painfully. If I could go back in time knowing everything I knew now, I would still marry Jeff because, without him, I wouldn't have Summer.

Headlights shined into the garage, and a moment later, Thatcher appeared at my door. He held up the pizza box, but his smile quickly faded when he saw my face.

Placing the pizza box on the hood of my car, he opened my door and leaned inside. "Everything okay?"

I swiped my hand across my cheek to dry my tears. "Fine," I said, feeling comforted by Thatcher's solid presence. His clean, woodsy scent, his reassuring smile, his strong, welcoming arms—he made everything better. "She fell asleep."

"Ah." He glanced at Summer, out cold in the passenger seat. "You want some help with her?"

I nodded, feeling too overwhelmed with emotion to speak. Thatcher leaned in and brushed his lips across mine, warm and reassuring. He smiled down at me, then backed out of the car and walked around to Summer's side.

He opened her door and eased her into his arms, securing her to his chest. With a fake groan, he hoisted her higher in his arms, grinning as he strode toward the house. I grabbed the pizza and opened the door for him, my heart in my throat as he carried my daughter inside.

"You don't have to take her all the way to her room," I said. "You can put her on the sofa."

He cocked his eyebrow at me and gestured at the sofa. It was the same one we'd fucked on earlier, and I would never forget that incredible orgasm, nor the others that followed.

"I'll take her to her room, where she'll be more comfortable."

He carried her up the stairs as if she weighed nothing and laid her gently on her bed. I slipped off her shoes and covered her with a quilt. Aslan jumped onto the bed and settled himself at her feet.

I kissed her forehead, then turned off her light and closed the door.

"Thank you."

"No problem." He pulled me into his arms. "Missed you," he said, sliding his hands up my back to tug playfully at my ponytail.

I laughed, feeling lighter than I had since that morning when he'd rolled out of my bed. "It's only been a few hours."

He covered my mouth with his, a quick claiming kiss. "You hungry?"

I quirked a brow at him, not sure if he meant for dinner or him. The answer was both. "Starved."

His grin appeared, and he sighed. "I'm dying for pizza, but I'll have to settle for watching you eat it."

"What? Why?"

"I'm on a strict chicken-and-rice diet for the next few weeks." He groaned. "Beckett's idea."

"Beckett? My brother?"

"There's only one Beckett I know. Super-tall dude with glasses and a know-it-all attitude?"

I giggled. "That's him."

"He's ordered a meal delivery service for me so I can cut weight," Thatcher said. "Chicken and rice delivered right to my door for the next two weeks before weigh-in."

I stared up at him. "You're serious about this?"

His brow creased. "Of course."

"You don't need to lose weight. You're absolutely perfect." He was more than perfect. His golden-brown hair, chiseled jaw, and lean body were enough to fuel fantasies. Not to mention his heart. His extra-large, willing heart.

He cupped my face and leaned down to kiss me. "Thanks, babe. But I've got to get stronger if I want a shot at beating Malone." He led the way down the hall. "Let me watch you eat pizza, and I will be forever grateful."

I grabbed his hand and linked our fingers. "It's the least I can do."

Twenty-Three

They were all talking at once. The noise level grew as their voices soared over each other to be heard. Usually I looked forward to our monthly book club meetings, but tonight, the women of the Blue Ridge Book Club were giving me a headache.

I was working with sleep deprivation, sore muscles, and a serious craving for a large, greasy pizza.

"Yo!" I called out, rubbing my temples. "If you don't shut the fuck up, I'm getting another man in the club pronto."

They fell quiet almost immediately. Nothing worked better than the threat of bringing another man into our sacred book club.

"If you bring another man in, I'm out," Mia said. "This is my only man-free zone."

I cleared my throat. "Excuse me."

"You don't count, Thatcher," Lacey said, patting my shoulder. "You have a Tweety Bird tattoo."

"It was after boot camp," I said, pushing her hand away.

"I've had it with men," Sloane said. "The last date I went on, the man tried to take me to the airport to watch the planes land. I think he wanted to kill me."

"That's a make-out spot," Gabi said.

"How do you know?" I asked.

"I have a teenager."

Kennedy held up her book, a thick tome set in Russia during World War One. "I want to have lunch with this author," she said. "So I can poison him."

Those were strong words coming from Kennedy, the chillest person I knew. She owned a yoga studio and ran wellness retreats. Poison was not in her vocabulary. "Must have been a horrible book," I said.

"Nah. It was freaking amazing."

"So why do you want to commit a crime?" Mia asked, sounding like the solicitor she was.

"Because the sequel was due out seven years ago." Kennedy dropped the book on the table with a thud. "Seven years and he can't write another book? Beckett writes two a year, and he's CEO of a corporation."

"Beckett doesn't sleep," Lacey said.

"Neither does his sister." The words slipped out of my mouth before I could stop them. Every head swiveled in my direction, and I backtracked as quickly as possible, going to stand behind the counter of the cafe. "Anyone want coffee? I finally learned how to make a latte."

"Your lattes suck," Lacey said.

"I just need practice." I ducked behind the espresso machine and fiddled with the cups, hoping they would go back to chattering and forget my mention of Pressly. I found the power button and pressed it. Nothing happened.

"Scoot over, Boss Man." Lacey knocked her hip into mine. "Who wants a latte?"

Gabi raised her hand as if she was in class. "Make mine with nonfat milk."

"It's too late for caffeine," Sloane said. "I'll have wine."

"Thank fuck," I muttered. "Something I can do." I reached

into the cooler and pulled out a bottle of white wine. "Chardonnay okay?"

"My favorite."

While Lacey worked on the lattes, I poured Sloane a glass of wine and grabbed myself a sparkling water. No alcohol until after my fight—Jay's orders.

Mia stared me down as I popped the top on my can. "So, what's with you and Beckett's sister?"

"You're obviously into her," Sloane said, wiggling her eyebrows. "And she's into you, too."

"What makes you say that?" I took a long pull of my drink, trying not to give away exactly *how* into each other we were.

"Her calendar is still on February," Sloane said, giggling.

"We have a bit of a history," I admitted. Recent history if I counted last night.

"So we heard," said Kennedy.

The way the five of them were ganging up on me made me even more determined to add a man into the mix.

"Yeah, we heard all about your teenage adventures. You dog," Lacey said.

I was tired of being on the hot seat. "What do you guys think of Jay? He might be a nice addition to the book club."

Mia scoffed. "That meathead doesn't read anything but the label on protein powder."

"You'd be surprised," I said.

"He's nice eye candy," Sloane said.

"I love that dragon tattoo he has across his bicep." Lacey's eyes lit up. "I bet it took at least five hours in the chair."

"Let's get this meeting going," Gabi said. "I'm on a tight schedule."

"What do you have? A hot date?" Mia asked.

Gabi's face flushed. "Of course not. You know I don't date."

"So why do you look all hot and bothered?" Lacey asked, handing her the nonfat latte.

"It's hot in here." Gabi fanned her face with her book, which featured a demonic-looking dude with tattoos straddling a motorcycle.

"Maybe it's that book," I told Gabi. "You go first."

Ours wasn't a traditional book club where we all read the same book every month. Instead, we read and reviewed our own genres, then got together to discuss.

Mia came to stand beside me at the counter. "You okay?" she asked quietly.

I nodded, focusing my attention on Gabi as she expounded on the motorcycle club hero she'd been reading about.

"How's your training?" she asked, pinning me with her inquisitive gaze. Mia was a tiny powerhouse. She never gave up once she got started on something, and it was impossible to hide anything from her.

"It's fine," I said.

"It better be, considering your opponent."

At Mia's announcement, everyone fell silent and turned to me.

"What?" I shrugged. "So, he's TikTok famous. That doesn't mean he can box."

Gabi pulled up Logan Malone's most recent video for social media.

His hair was shaved into a Mohawk style, and tattoos covered his torso. He was hitting a speed bag at an alarming rate, glaring like he was going to plow through a brick wall.

My stomach clenched as I watched his fists pound into the bag.

"Gee whiz," Lacey said, concern in her voice. "He's gonna kill you."

I shifted uncomfortably. "Thanks for the vote of confidence."

She shrugged. "Sorry, pal, but it's true."

"At least he'll bring a good crowd," I said. As Sloane scrolled through his videos, I saw how many likes and views he got. "It will be great publicity for the gym."

"Speaking of publicity," Sloane said. "You need some help."

"I've got a press conference and a photo shoot scheduled."

"You should have told me," she said. "I can get the Walled Garden for your photo shoot." She squinted. "It would make for some killer promo. The boxer in the vineyard garden, surrounded by ivy and flowers with the Blue Ridge Mountains at his back."

"I like it," Kennedy said. "But you need some baby goats in there."

Mia snickered. "Baby goats?"

Kennedy nodded. "Everyone loves baby goats."

"You should get a wind machine," Lacey said, flipping my hair. "Just picture this flowing mane à la Fabio."

Gabi wiggled her eyebrows. "You should wear those silky blue shorts. It would make a great book cover for a boxing romance."

"Give me a break," I groaned.

Mia saved me by launching into a synopsis of the thriller she'd just read. The book club was back on track, but I was hardly listening. The video of Logan Malone was stuck on replay in my mind. His fists were fast. Faster than any of the videos I'd watched of him fighting.

I'd never seen fists so fast in my life. Maybe the video was speeded up.

I grabbed my phone and texted Jay, asking him what the fuck I'd just seen.

For the first time since I'd volunteered to fight, fear pricked my chest. I wasn't as scared of Malone as much as I was scared of myself.

If I froze up in the ring like I had last time, fists as fast as those could do some serious damage.

"Hey," Lacey said, nudging my arm. "Where'd you go?"

"I'm right here." I forced a smile. "I'm not going anywhere."

Twenty-Four

"Can I help you find something?" A deep male voice sounded behind me.

I stopped abruptly and turned around, coming face to chest with an exceptionally tall man. As I lifted my gaze up his impressive muscles to his face, a chill ran down my spine. He was so striking, I was stunned into silence. His dark blue eyes scrutinized me with an intensity that left me feeling completely exposed. His jaw flexed, a muscle ticking behind his tanned skin. "The self-defense class is in Studio B," he said.

"Self-defense class?"

His eyes narrowed. "Is that what you're looking for?"

"No. I'm here for my daughter." I gestured at the group of young kids gathered by the long wall of mirrors at the back of the gym. "It's her first time at Champion's Corner."

"Ah," he said, checking his clipboard. "You must be Mrs. Carleton."

"Vinroot-Carleton," I corrected, more out of habit than anything else. Maybe it was time to change my name for good. The hyphenated name had always been a pain, and now there was no reason to carry it any longer. I couldn't get Jeff out of my life completely, but I could get rid of his name.

"Summer fits in well with the group," Jay said, his gruff demeanor slipping as his gaze focused on the kids.

I followed his gaze to my daughter and was struck by the look of fierce determination on her face as she jumped rope. She reminded me so much of Beckett sometimes. Her hair was lighter than his dark brown, but they shared the same expressive eyes and stubborn chin. Beckett had always been determined to accomplish his goals no matter what got in his way, and Summer was the same.

"There's plenty of room in the class, and your daughter won't be finished for almost another hour."

I checked the time on my phone. I hadn't meant to be so early, but I was curious about the gym where Thatcher spent so much of his time. I'd been hoping to catch a glimpse of him training.

Gesturing down at my slim skirt and high heels, I smiled. "I don't have on the right clothes."

A slight smile curved his mouth, somehow making him look even more dangerous. "You can't rely on being dressed to fight when a threat comes at you," he said. His voice was a deep rumble coming from his wide chest. He pointed at my high heels. "Those are an asset. Think of the damage you could do if you stepped on your assailant's foot."

I lifted my foot and eyed the spiky heel. The shoes had been a very expensive gift to myself when my divorce became final. I'd never thought of them as a weapon, but he was right—they were potentially dangerous.

"The classes are free," he continued. "All you have to do is sign this waiver." He flipped through the pages on his clipboard until he found what he needed.

I cocked my head at him, recognizing a sales pitch. "Do you get a bonus when people sign up or something?"

"Nah." He shook his head. "But I am the owner of this place." His gaze scanned the bustling gym with obvious pride, and then he held his hand out to me. "Jay Sanchez."

"Ah," I said. "So you're Jay. I'm Pressly. It's nice to meet you." I shook his hand, matching his firm grip.

"And you're the neighbor who has been occupying Thatcher."

My eyebrows lifted. "Occupying him?"

"If Thatcher has a prayer to win this fight, he needs to focus." He pinned me with a scrutinizing gaze. "You're a distraction he doesn't need right now."

A knot formed in my stomach. "You don't think he can win?"

"I didn't say that. Of course he can win."

I folded my arms over my chest. "He's a good fighter, right?"

Jay shrugged. "He's quick on his feet and packs a lot of heat in his punch."

"But?" I sensed there was more coming.

"No buts," Jay said after a moment of hesitation. "He'll take down the Hitman if he sets his mind to it."

"The Hitman?" I asked, cringing.

"That's what they call him."

"Why? Is he in the mafia?"

Jay laughed. "No, but it only takes one punch to make his opponent crumble."

My chest squeezed as I pictured Thatcher crumbling. I knew I'd never be able to watch the fight.

"Is he here?" I asked, sweeping my gaze around the crowded gym.

"If you want to see Thatcher, you should sign up for self-defense class."

My eyebrows shot up. "Wow. You're really pushing this class, aren't you?"

"Nothing wrong with learning to defend yourself," he said, flipping a page on the clipboard and handing it to me. "Plus, I think you'll like the teacher."

I signed the waiver, then headed to the class in Studio B. As soon as I walked in and saw the instructor, pleasure jolted through my system, and a slow smile spread over my face.

Thatcher stood at the head of the class, looking particularly yummy in a fitted tank and athletic shorts. His hands were on his hips in a powerful stance that said he was clearly the one in charge.

Although I'd come to the gym early to see him in action, I wasn't prepared for the emotions swirling through me.

Since our marathon night of sex, I hadn't seen Thatcher in public. Seeing him in a group setting with a dozen women staring at him, a wave of possessiveness crashed over me. I had the uncontrollable urge to march up to him and lay claim to him in front of everyone.

His gaze traveled over the students, suddenly skidding to a halt on me. A sexy smile curved his mouth, but it was the look in his eyes that lit me up inside. He was looking at me the same way I was looking at him, as if he wanted to kiss me in front of the entire room.

"Welcome, everyone," he said to the class, but his blue eyes told me I was the only one who mattered. "I'm glad you're here."

Warmth spread through me under the glow of his gaze. My heart squeezed, and the growing emotions for him pulsed with a life of their own. The realization struck me that I was in love with this man.

Maybe I'd never stopped loving him.

Clearly comfortable in his role as teacher, Thatcher addressed the room full of women. "In a perfect world, women wouldn't need to learn self-defense because men wouldn't create bad situations," he said.

"Amen!" called a voice from behind me. Grumbles of agreement from the others followed.

"We're going to start with a few basics that will help you learn how to take control when you're in danger. You won't need strength to perform these moves, but you will need confidence and a clear head. I encourage you to practice these drills until they are second nature so if the time comes when you need to use them, you won't panic."

I watched him with hungry eyes, devouring every inch of his delicious body in his workout clothes. Memories of Thatcher walking naked up the stairs to my bedroom flashed through my mind, making it hard to concentrate on what he was saying.

"Come here, Pressly."

My thoughts cleared as he said my name, and I snapped to attention.

"What?"

"We are going to start in pairs," he said, reaching for my hand. "You're with me."

Twenty-Five

"Those shoes might be a problem." I pointed at Pressly's feet.

"Jay said they might come in handy during an altercation."

I rolled my eyes. Of course Jay had said that, but there was no way I was being impaled by a stiletto. "This is just training."

"You're afraid of my shoes?"

"Definitely." I had a boxing match to think about. I couldn't afford to get injured by an ice pick to the foot.

"Then you have to take yours off, too," she said. "So we're even."

I toed off my sneakers and stripped out of my socks, then lifted a brow at her. "Your turn."

I hadn't meant for it to sound sexy, but the blush spreading up Pressly's neck confirmed she'd heard the teasing tone in my voice.

She stepped out of her high heels and was instantly the perfect size to tuck under my chin. A low hum of awareness spread through my body as I inhaled the subtle fragrance of her perfume. She always smelled so good I wanted to devour her.

I had plans for that later.

I glanced around the class at the women who'd divided themselves into pairs. They were chatting and laughing, completely unaware of the sexual current sparking between me and Pressly.

I turned my attention to them, sweeping my gaze over the room to make sure everyone had a partner. "You ladies ready to have some fun?" I asked.

"Show us how to kick some ass," one of them yelled from the back of the room.

Laughter rang out as the others joined in with encouragement. These women were out for blood.

"The first thing we are going to learn is how to get out of an arm grab." I motioned for Pressly to come closer. "Grab me by the wrist," I told her.

When her cool fingers slipped around my wrist, the jolt was like a rush of pure adrenaline. Maybe it had been a mistake to make her my partner. Her touch did crazy things to my system, and I had a class to teach.

I forced myself to focus.

"Your first instinct is going to be to run away, but you have to shut that down. Don't panic. Don't run. Instead, take control. The goal is to get away, not stay and fight."

I gripped her hand, swung my arm around hers, and pushed her down to her knees. She stared up at me with a shocked expression, and the room burst into applause.

I helped her to her feet, ignoring the fire shooting from her eyes. "Now you try it," I said. "We'll go through it again slowly."

I grabbed Pressly's arm, and she put her hand on top of mine just like I'd shown her, but instead of flipping my arm, she turned on me. I saw the wild look in her eyes a moment before her fist came out and slammed into my face.

Waves of pain shot through me, and then I felt the warm gush of blood pouring from my nose.

"Oh, my God!" Pressly said. "I'm so sorry!"

I cupped my hands over my nose, trying to stem the flow of

blood, and suddenly, the room began to fade. The metallic taste of blood filled my mouth, and I saw red.

Blood was everywhere. It soaked the leaves on the trees, covered the forest floor, and dripped from my hands.

"Thatcher?" Pressly's voice sounded from far away. "Are you okay?"

Alarm bells rang in my head.

My skin crawled as if an invisible army of ants was marching over me, and my throat closed. The sounds of distant screams grew louder in my head, and I knew what was waiting for me.

No air. No thoughts. A dark hole of despair.

An arm came around my waist and supported my weight as my knees buckled. "You're okay. I've got you."

The last thing I saw was Pressly's big blue eyes swimming with tears. And then total blackness.

* * *

A cool cloth bathed my face. The ringing in my ears gave way to the sound of a soft voice near my ear.

"It's okay. You're safe now."

I opened my eyes, wincing at the bright overhead light. Blinking slowly, I saw Pressly leaning over me.

There was no jungle. No burning village. No screaming victims.

I was in Jay's office, which explained the stench of liniment and dirty socks.

Pressly's eyes widened, tears glistening as she gazed down at me. "You're back," she said.

I closed my eyes, hoping to ward off the headache that always came after one of my episodes.

"I'm fine," I said, dragging in a deep breath.

"You're not fine," Pressly said, dabbing my forehead with the cloth.

I pushed her hand away and tried to sit up. "I need to get back to class."

"No." She pressed her hand to my chest, urging me to lie back down on the sofa. "Jay's in there. He took over."

I winced. "Jay's horrible with the clients."

Her fingers sifted through my hair. It felt so good I lay back on the sofa and let her touch me.

"Want to tell me what the hell just happened?" she asked.

I smiled a little. "Your right cross is what just happened," I said. "You pack quite a punch. You should think about getting in the ring."

"I'm sorry about that," she said, her voice breaking. "I was thinking about Jeff, picturing his smug face... I didn't mean to hurt you."

I reached for her hand. "It was nothing," I said.

"That was *not* nothing." She pulled her hand away. "Something happened after I punched you. You completely shut down." She poked a finger at my chest. "You were gone, Thatcher. Checked out."

I sat up, grunting from the exertion. The ache in my head threatened to split me open. "Nothing happened."

A pained expression crossed her face, drawing her brows together. "What if *nothing* happens again when you're in the ring?"

I forced a smile. "It won't. I can take a punch. You just caught me off guard."

"What if your opponent catches you off guard?"

I gnashed my teeth, anger mounting in my chest. "I should get back to class before Jay scares away all the clients."

Pressly stared up at me, her face a mask of confusion and pain. "You think you should fight?"

My jaw clenched. "Of course I can fight."

"I didn't ask if you could," she said, narrowing her eyes at me. "I asked if you should. Has this ever happened to you before?"

I avoided her gaze, unable to lie. "You don't understand."

"Explain it, then."

"Don't worry," I said, sitting down next to her. "I've got this under control."

Getting in the ring was a risk, but it was a risk I had to take. Not only for the gym but for myself. I had to prove I was in control and that the past had no power over me.

I placed my hand on her leg, my fingers brushing her skin where her skirt met her knee. "Support me on this?"

She laced our fingers together, her hand warm on my clammy palm. "I want to support you," she said. "You know I do. But you shouldn't fight."

I stiffened, pulling my hand away. "I have to."

"Why?"

"Everyone is counting on me. The gym could go under without me taking this fight."

"Why should you risk your life?" Her voice erupted angrily.

My head pounded, blood roaring between my ears. "You're being dramatic," I said.

"Oh my God." She stood abruptly. "I'm dramatic? You're the one taking this gym on your back."

"It has to be me." My voice cracked under the strain.

She shook her head. "Why?"

"Because if I don't fight—" I paused, then blurted out the words I didn't want to admit. "I'll never know if I can."

She stared down at me, eyes shining, lips parted. "You shouldn't fight," she said. "And if you do, don't expect me to be there to watch the debacle."

Her angry declaration hung in the air as she strode out of the office, slamming the door behind her.

Twenty-Six

I'd always dreamed I'd have a home filled to the brim with family and friends during the holidays, and we would all gather in the kitchen.

We would cook big dinners, bake cookies, and gossip about everyone we knew.

I didn't have the big family and cozy kitchen I'd always wanted, but I did have the restaurant at Sky Valley Resort.

The five-star restaurant was the heart and soul of the resort. It was where everyone hung out between shifts, ate delicious food, and spilled the tea on everyone in town.

I'd chosen my tiny office because it was near the kitchen.

I didn't need a fancy office to do my job as manager—I could fill out spreadsheets anywhere—but I did need the hive of the kitchen to fuel my soul.

Not only did the proximity of my hole-in-the-wall office allow me to know what the employees were up to, but it also gave me a window to the guests.

Sky Valley attracted the rich and famous. Since it opened in 1925, Sky Valley Resort had welcomed presidents, royals, and countless celebrities.

It was why we needed a world-class chef to put his signature style on the dishes. I'd stolen Giovanni Massimiliano from a restaurant in Atlanta, thinking he would put a modern spin on the old-fashioned menu. And he had, but he was also a diva who was incredibly hard to work with. He insisted on cooking food that he was proud of and often complained about the guests' preferences.

"I will not boil chicken!"

Giovanni's voice boomed from the kitchen.

"Come on, Gio," one of the servers whined. "You're gonna ruin my tip. Put on your big-boy pants and boil some damn chicken."

A loud crash sounded, followed by a string of curses. "Boiled chicken and steamed rice with no seasonings!" Another bang. "No spices!" A crash of metal against metal. "It's a crime!"

I froze in place, my fingers hovering over my keyboard. Boiled chicken and steamed rice reminded me of Thatcher. It was all he could eat leading up to the dreaded fight. He'd eaten it dutifully while watching me devour greasy pizza right in front of him.

Frustration knotted in my belly. Thatcher and I hadn't spoken since the disastrous self-defense class.

I missed him terribly, but I was too proud to seek him out. Plus, I was busy, absolutely swamped with spreadsheets and all sorts of other things.

The resort was hosting a celebrity wedding in a few weeks, and I needed to check in with Sloane and make sure everything was on schedule.

My father didn't take me seriously as manager of the resort, but this wedding could change that.

I left my office and walked through the kitchen. It was the middle of the day, and everyone was in prep mode for the night shift. Music piped over the speakers, servers stood at stations rolling silverware, and cooks prepared ingredients.

The laughter and chatter gave me the warm feeling of home. I loved being around the staff. They were like an extended family.

"He's fucking hot as hell," one of the servers said as she sorted silverware. "Maybe he needs someone to cut his chicken and feed it to him."

"Or help him change out of those silky shorts," one of the cooks chimed in.

"Did you know he was Mr. February?"

"So fucking hot."

I froze beside the silverware station, blatantly eavesdropping. When the staff noticed me, the conversation halted.

"Hi, Mrs. Vinroot-Carleton."

The kitchen went silent as everyone turned to look at me. Still a newcomer, I hadn't quite earned the trust of the staff yet. Their previous boss had been a real dick, and they were wary of managers.

"It's Pressly," I reminded them. "Mrs. Vinroot-Carleton is too much of a mouthful." Which reminded me I needed to remedy that. "Good job with the luncheon today," I said, trying to ease the awkwardness with compliments. "Everyone was raving about the food and service."

"Thank you, ma'am," one of the servers said.

Giovanni's voice bellowed from behind the counter. "Your tasteless chicken and boring rice dish is ready, Kat!"

Kat dropped the roll of silverware in the pile and turned to get the food.

Curiosity sparked in my chest. "Is that for room service?"

"No, it's for the photo shoot in the vineyard." She placed a silver dome over the dish and loaded it on a tray. "Special request."

My heart slammed against my ribs. "Photo shoot?"

"For Fight Night," she said. "They're doing it in the vineyard. It's very artsy."

"Oh." I fell into step beside her as she hoisted the tray. "I was just about to do my rounds. Maybe I should check it out."

She gave me a sideways look, clearly not comfortable with her boss following her around. "Okay," she said, leading the way outside to the vineyards. "Are you going to Fight Night?" she asked.

I swallowed the lump in my throat. "Are you?"

"If I can get my shift covered," she said. "I usually work Saturday nights."

I nodded, trying to remain casual as we strolled through the walled garden towards an ivy-covered gazebo strung with lights and flowers. Framed by the dramatic backdrop of the Blue Ridge Mountains, it was the perfect spot to get married—or hold a photo shoot for a boxing match.

A table of props sat under the shady grove of hemlocks, and crew members rushed around setting the stage. Boxing gloves among the blooming flowers should have been an odd sight, but the juxtaposition worked. A play on hard and soft, it romanticized the event.

And then there was Thatcher. The sight of Thatcher in his boxing shorts, bare-chested and smiling, sent flutters through my belly.

God, he was gorgeous.

His hands were wrapped with tape, and his lean, muscled chest glistened with artificial sweat. They'd set up a huge fan that made his hair blow and the silky blue shorts stick to his powerful thighs.

Arousal tugged low in my core, and I couldn't tear my eyes from him. If the fight could be one with sex appeal, Thatcher would be unbeatable.

A chill ran down my spine at the thought of Thatcher lying broken and beaten in the ring. The image stole my breath, and I paused for a moment, dragging in air.

His reason for fighting nearly broke my heart. He was the type of man who wanted to fix things for others. Not only sinks but broken hearts and failing gyms.

But saving the gym might get him hurt or worse.

There had to be some way to convince him not to fight.

An idea lodged in my mind. Maybe there was a way around it. If the gym needed saving, Fight Night might not be the only way to do it.

One of the crew members rubbed Thatcher's chest with a cloth, and he looked up at her, saying something that made her laugh. The fan caught the long, silky strands of his hair, blowing it back from his face.

"Lord Almighty," Kat said on a wistful sigh. "I think I just got pregnant."

I bit back a sigh of my own, trying not to picture Thatcher on top of me, holding me down to the bed as he stroked his thick cock in and out of me.

Determined to remain professional, I plastered on a smile and greeted the camera crew. The director was a tall, curvaceous woman dressed in a designer outfit that looked like it had been poured onto her. Her hair and makeup were perfect enough to be on the other side of the camera.

"Hello," I said, extending my hand. "I'm Pressly Vinroot-Carleton, manager of the resort. If you need anything, please let me know."

Her smile flashed, and she took my hand in her soft, firm grip. "Cassandra Darling."

Her accent was low-country, upper-class, the long vowels and dropped consonants calling up images of moss-covered oaks and sandy beaches.

"Thank you for letting us shoot here," she said. "It's the perfect location for Pretty Boy's image."

My whole body cringed at hearing Thatcher's nickname. "You're welcome."

His head turned, and his gaze caught mine. Tension throbbed between us, thick enough to choke on before he looked away, saying something else to make the assistant laugh.

The photographer directed Thatcher to sit on a bench in the gazebo, and a woman dressed as a ring girl in a string bikini strutted over to perch on his lap. His arm came up around her waist, and he pressed his lips to her cheek. Lust sparked in the bikini girl's eyes, and whether or not it was just for the camera suddenly didn't matter.

Jealousy flared in my chest, and I tore my gaze away, unable to watch any longer.

"Excuse me," I said. "I should get back to work."

"Me too," Cassandra said. "It was nice meeting you. Maybe we can work together again. I'd love to do some events here."

"Yes." I backed away, aiming my gaze anywhere but the sensual scene in the gazebo. "Of course. Sounds wonderful."

I retraced my steps back to the hotel, barely looking where I was going. I had no right to be jealous—Thatcher wasn't mine. We'd had sex a few times—that didn't mean we were dating. He could kiss whoever he wanted. And so could I.

The problem was I didn't want to kiss anyone else. I wanted Thatcher.

"Pressly?" The front desk clerk called my name as I walked through the lobby.

"Yes, Mary Maxwell?" I stopped at the desk, the fire of jealousy still raging in my belly.

"Can you talk to James about his bathroom breaks?" she asked.

"Um." I held in a sigh of frustration. "Bathroom breaks?"

Mary Maxwell opened the desk drawer and pulled out a sheet of paper filled with hand-written notes.

"I wrote down all the 'bathroom breaks' he took yesterday. It's unacceptable." Her brows pulled together in suspicion. "What is he doing in the bathroom for so long?"

I skimmed the paper, my mind still stuck on Thatcher and the bikini-clad model. "I'll look into it."

"Maybe you should send him to the pool and get Marshall back on the front desk," she suggested.

I folded the paper and tucked it into the pocket of my blazer. "I promise I'll look into it."

I walked through the kitchen back to my office with a purposeful stride, determined to put Thatcher out of my mind.

Twenty-Seven

As soon as we wrapped up the photo shoot, I wiped the oil off my chest, changed into my street clothes, and sweet-talked the clerk at the front desk into telling me where to find Pressly.

Tucked between the walk-in coolers and a supply closet, Pressly's office was not what I expected for the manager of the resort.

Her door was partially open, and I knocked as I stepped inside.

She looked up as I entered. Her eyes widened in surprise when she saw me, and for a moment, she just stared. Then, her chin poked out, and her eyes narrowed.

It wasn't the warm welcome I'd been hoping for, but we hadn't exactly left things tidy between us. She'd been avoiding me since our argument over the fight, and I'd been respectful, giving her some space, but I could only be patient for so long.

"Can I come in?" I asked.

She shrugged, her gaze focused on her computer screen. "You're already in," she said.

That surprised a chuckle from me. "Yeah. So I am."

I glanced around her office, noticing it was neat and tidy, just like Pressly. A little stuffy, though. With no windows and filing cabinets lining three of the walls, it gave me claustrophobic vibes.

Closing the door behind me, I took a seat in the chair across from her. She looked classy and sophisticated in her work clothes, with her hair pinned in a neat twist at the nape of her neck.

"You ran off before I could say hello at the photo shoot."

She didn't look up but tapped her bottom lip with her pen, making a quick note in a folder on her desk. "You seemed to have your hands full," she said, sparing me a scathing glance. "How did you get back here, anyway?"

"It wasn't that hard," I said. "I just asked the clerk at the front desk."

Her eyes turned flat and hard. "I'll have to speak with the staff about telling strangers the location of my office."

My jaw clenched. "Stranger?" We'd left things badly, but this was something more than a disagreement over the fight. "Pressly?" I leaned forward, watching her closely. Her face was flushed, and her chest rose and fell as she breathed heavily. "What's up?"

She glared at me, eyes firing daggers. "I wasn't expecting to see you—" She gestured up and down my body, her gaze disapproving. "Like that."

"Like what?"

She exhaled a frustrated breath charged with electricity. "Half-naked with a woman draped over you."

My brows rose, and my shoulders inched up to my ears. "It was a photo shoot," I said. "She was a model."

Pressly huffed. "A barely clothed model."

The tension in my shoulders relaxed as I realized where this was coming from. Her anger had nothing to do with the argument we'd had. "You're jealous."

She sighed and returned her attention to her computer. "I'm not jealous. I'm just busy."

I sat back in the chair, and my gaze caught on the calendar pinned to the wall behind her desk. It was the Men of Mossy Oak calendar—opened to February.

Reaching forward, I caught her fingers, refusing to back down. "Come over to my place when you get off work."

Two spots of color appeared on her cheeks, and she pulled her hand back. "I can't."

I stood and walked around to her side of the desk, standing so close she couldn't ignore me. "Why not?"

"I can't just drop everything to be with you," she said, swallowing hard as I stalked closer, invading her space. "I have a daughter." She tipped her head back as I loomed over her. "Responsibilities."

I placed my hands on the arms of her chair, caging her in. "What about right now?" I asked. "Do you have time for me now?"

Her eyes flashed, and her lips parted. The little sigh escaping her mouth spurred me on.

"Do you know what I wanted to do when I saw you in this sexy little skirt?" My hand went to the hem of her skirt, and I inched it up her leg. "You're a hundred times hotter than that girl in the bikini."

Her breath hitched as I pushed her skirt up higher, her eyes darkening so that the black of her pupils took over the blue of her eyes.

Grabbing her hand, I placed it over the bulge in my jeans. "Feel that?" I asked.

Her tongue peeked out from her mouth to touch her bottom lip.

"That's for you. No one else."

It was sad but true. The scantily dressed ring girl didn't do it for me, but Pressly in her buttoned-up blouse, blazer, and classy skirt made me hard as steel.

Trailing my hand up her skirt, I lightly brushed her over her panties. She trembled and opened her legs slightly, allowing me to drag her panties to the side.

"You're wet for me already," I said, awed by how little it took for us to turn each other on.

Her hand stroked over my straining cock, and the little noise of appreciation she made drove me wild.

I pushed one finger through her wetness, and she let her head fall back on a moan. I leaned down and kissed the exposed column of her neck, trailing a hot path to her lips.

Our mouths crashed together, our tongues meeting in a fiery match.

All the jealousy and frustration from our argument writhed between us. I kissed her hard, desperate to soothe the ache inside me. She kissed me back harder, her hand sliding up and over my cock as I fucked her with my fingers.

"Thatcher?"

"Yeah."

"Lock the door."

I didn't waste time obeying her command. I locked her door, then stalked back to her desk.

"What do you want now?"

She gave me a look full of heat and hunger. "I want you."

"Yes, sweetheart. I want you, too." I dropped to my knees in front of her chair. Gripping her hips, I yanked her forward. "But I want to hear you say exactly what you want from me. Can you do that?"

She squirmed in the chair and nodded.

"What else do you want?"

She hiked her skirt up her thighs and pulled down her panties. A furious blush stained her cheeks.

I eased her thighs further apart. "Ask for what you want," I said, placing a kiss on her knee. "And I'll give it to you."

She bit into her lower lip, her eyes devouring me. "I want you to kiss me." She widened her legs, exposing her glistening pussy. "Here."

"Good girl," I said with approval. Bending my head to the task, I inhaled the scent of her arousal. Then, I gripped her hips and dragged her to my face, giving her a long, slow lick.

She squirmed against me, a muffled moan escaping her

mouth. I looked up to see she had her fist in her mouth, her eyes locked on me.

I flashed a grin at her. "I've been wanting to do this," I said, spreading her open so I could taste her again. I took my time with her, licking long and deep and then sucking the swollen nub of her clit until she writhed against me.

Her fingers tangled in my hair, and she held me in place as she moaned my name.

"Yes," she panted, clutching her legs around my ears as I swirled my tongue over her clit and then plunged it deep.

I added my finger, stroking into her slick pussy in a steady rhythm until she came with a long, shuddering sigh.

When she was still, I sat back on my heels and wiped my mouth with the back of my hand. She watched me with hooded eyes, tracking my every move.

I popped open the button on my jeans and reached for my zipper. "Got any condoms in here?"

She grinned. "As a matter of fact, I do."

A knock on the door startled us both.

We froze, and then Pressly sprang into action. She straightened her skirt and smoothed her hair. "You need to get out of here."

I cocked a brow at her. "Where do you want me to go?"

"Pressly?" called the voice at the door. "Are you in there?"

I recognized Sloane's voice and rolled my eyes. The entire book club was going to know my business now.

"I'll be right there," Pressly said, combing her hair back into a tidy twist.

"Come over tonight," I said, fastening my jeans and adjusting myself.

"It might be late," she said.

"I don't care what time. Just come."

The doorknob rattled, and Pressly hurried to answer it.

"It's just Sloane," I said. "She's a friend."

She gave me a pointed look. "I'm her boss."

When Pressly opened the door, Sloane strode in, freezing when she saw me. Her gaze flew to Pressly, and her green eyes went wide.

"Hey, Sloane," I said.

She blinked a few times, and then a smug smile appeared on her lips. With a twinkle in her eyes, she said, "Hello, Thatcher. Or should I call you Pretty Boy?"

I curled my lip at her. "Don't even think about it."

Sloane giggled, not bothering to hide her delight in my discomfort.

Ignoring her, I reached for Pressly. She shot me a surprised look but didn't protest as I kissed her. After a moment, she even kissed me back.

I released her, wondering how she liked the taste of herself on my lips. There was a lot more where that came from. "See you tonight."

Twenty-Eight

After dropping Summer off at the airport, I drove home in an angry fog. Jeff had said they were going to Charleston again, for a food truck festival this time, and I'd played dumb.

It didn't matter what he said; I didn't believe a word he said. But I did want to smash my fist into his lying mouth, just once.

Maybe I could get Thatcher to teach me how to throw a proper punch. Not one born out of anger and frustration.

Ah... Thatcher. The thought of him made me forget my anger at my asshole ex-husband.

My body still tingled from his touch, and thinking of him sparked a longing I couldn't ignore.

When I knocked on his front door, he opened it right away and pulled me into his arms. I laughed and looped my arms around his neck as he dragged me into his house.

"Were you standing at the door?" I asked, giggling as he nuzzled my neck.

"Sure was." He cinched his arm around my waist and then hoisted me over his shoulder.

"Oh my God!" I hung over his shoulder, slapping lightly at his back as he strode through the living room. "What are you doing?"

"I'm not letting you get away," he said, carrying me straight up the stairs. "I want you in my bed."

A thrill of excitement shot through me as I dangled over his shoulder, watching the stairs give way to a long hall.

We entered his bedroom, and he bent to deposit me on the floor. "Nice," I said, taking a quick look around.

His bedroom looked exactly as I'd pictured it. Decorated with clean lines and soothing colors, the space radiated quiet strength and masculinity, just like Thatcher.

"Thanks." He reached behind him and pulled his shirt over his head, tossing it to the ground. "Off." A wicked smile curved his lips as he pointed to my clothes.

"Not wasting any time, are you?" I could see the outline of his cock through his jeans. Hard and thick, it pressed against the denim in the most delicious way. I wanted to touch it, taste it, ride it.

He saw where I was looking and popped open the button on his jeans. "Want this?" he asked, teasing his zipper down.

I couldn't drag my eyes away as he unzipped his jeans and his cock snapped into his hand, long and magnificent. No underwear.

My body pulsed to life, liquid slicking between my thighs.

He pushed his jeans down, standing fully naked in front of me, his dick proud and angry between his legs, beading at the tip with precum. His body was perfect. Broad chest, defined six-pack, and a deep V pointing to his thick, eager shaft.

Feeling suddenly shy with all Thatcher had going on, I worried my bottom lip between my teeth.

"Hey." He stepped forward, cupping my face with both hands. "Do you remember telling me what you wanted today in your office?" he asked, his lips close to mine and his breath a soft puff against my lips.

Arousal sparked in my core, soaking my panties. He'd made me ask for him to go down on me, and it should have been mortifying, but it was... thrilling. "Yes," I breathed, opening my mouth as his tongue licked across the seam of my lips.

"Now it's my turn." His voice was a soft growl, lighting a fire inside me.

I reached for him, but he took a step back, fisting his hand around his impressive cock. He stroked it almost absently, his gaze a fiery brand on me.

"Take off your clothes," he said.

I reached for the buttons of my blouse, but he stopped me. "No." He gestured down. "Bottom first. I want to see your sweet pussy." He licked his lips. "I can still taste you."

Shit. I'd never been so turned on in my life. I didn't know I liked it dirty, but apparently, I was what my aunts referred to as a hussy.

I reached around and unzipped my skirt, letting it pool around my ankles. I stepped out of it, kicking off my heels.

Thatcher watched me, his eyes glazing over with lust. He nodded encouragingly as I hooked my thumbs in the sides of my panties and pulled them down my legs.

"Very nice," he said, spinning his finger in the air. "Turn around."

I did a slow spin. My blouse barely covered my ass, and the cool air felt good against my hot skin. He hadn't even touched me, and I was dripping wet, my inner thighs glistening.

"Fuck," he growled. "Now the top."

I fumbled with the buttons, feeling more empowered with each one I undid as his eyes feasted on me. Sliding my bra straps off my shoulders, I reached around and unclasped the hooks. My breasts spilled out, heavy and aching for his touch.

His gaze devoured my naked body, a flush rising up his neck.

I stood very still under his inspection, then found my voice. "What now?" I asked.

His sensual mouth curved in a wicked grin. "I want you to suck me off," he said. "Can you do that, Pressly?"

I nodded and knelt before him. Bracing my hands on his powerful thighs, I wet my lips and opened my mouth.

"Good girl," he said, his voice raw and hungry.

I flushed with pleasure. I didn't know I had a praise kink either. Apparently, I was full of surprises because hearing Thatcher say *Good girl* turned me into a throbbing bundle of need.

I wrapped my lips around him, wasting no time sucking him deep into the back of my throat.

His hips bucked, and he bit out a curse. He fisted his hand in my hair and pulled my head back, locking eyes with me as I swirled my tongue over his thick crown.

"Fuck," he growled. "This is too much."

I smiled around his cock, a surge of power vibrating through me. Sucking him deeper, I choked a little as he nudged the back of my throat. In long, teasing pulls, I worked my mouth over him.

His taste was intoxicating. Pure masculinity.

Thrusting his hips, he cupped the back of my head, using my mouth for his pleasure.

And then he pulled back, moving so suddenly I would have fallen forward if he hadn't grabbed me under the arms and pulled me up.

"Enough," he said, covering my mouth with his.

His tongue stroked into my mouth, the rasp of his beard scruff scraping against my jaw. He walked me backward until my legs hit the bed and then gave me a gentle push so I sprawled onto the mattress.

He looked down at me, a naughty glint in his eyes. "I want to lick your gorgeous tits and suck your sweet nipples."

I choked back a sob of desire. My breasts ached to be touched, my nipples painfully hard.

His hand skimmed up my waist, pausing just under my breast. Our eyes locked, and I knew he was waiting for my consent. Even when he was rawly masculine, there was something so heartbreakingly sweet about him. He made me want to wrap my arms around him and hold on tight.

"Yes," I panted, scooting back on the bed as he knelt between my thighs. "I want that, too."

He bent to cover my breasts with hot kisses, flicking his tongue over my nipples and sucking deep.

I threaded my fingers through his hair and clutched his head to my chest. His talented mouth fastened on one nipple, then the other. Using his knee to spread my legs wider, he stroked his hand up my thigh.

"Fuck," he said, pulling back to look at me. "You're drenched."

He palmed me, fingers warm and strong against my quivering flesh. I pushed against his hand, grinding shamelessly.

He grinned. "I need to taste you."

One long finger pushed inside me, finding a slow, steady rhythm in and out, tweaking my clit with his thumb in the same pattern he'd used at the portrait studio that had me coming in record time.

The delicious sensations built inside me until I felt the first warning ripples of an orgasm crashing over me. My pussy clenched, and Thatcher slipped his hand away.

"No, not yet," he said, blowing cool air across my peaked nipple. "When you come, you're going to do it on my fucking face. Then my cock."

A whimper of surprise escaped my mouth. I'd never had a man talk to me like this. It was filthy, dirty, and so hot I almost came before he fastened his mouth on my clit and sucked.

And then I did come. So much it should have been embarrassing.

When the last aftershocks were over, Thatcher lifted his head and pinned me with a glare so full of desire it was dangerous. My juices ran down his face, and he wiped his mouth against my thigh, his chin scraping my sensitive skin.

He grabbed a condom from the nightstand, tore it open with

his teeth, and rolled it on in one swift motion. Then he was inside me, stretching me, filling me until all I knew was him.

His taste, his smell, the feel of him inside me. He was everything.

"I missed you," he said against my ear.

Tears pricked behind my eyes as his words sank in. Everything I'd been missing these years became all too clear.

Thatcher and I were perfect together. Two halves that made a whole.

Twenty-Nine

"And that's when I moved to Atlanta," Pressly said, trailing her fingers down the center of my chest.

"Hmm." I hummed with pleasure as her nails gently scratched my skin. "I can't see you there. You belong in Mossy Oak."

She snuggled closer, her hair a soft cloud on my shoulder. "I like it here."

I cupped her shoulder, drawing her closer to press a kiss to her forehead. "I like you here, too."

"And you?" She raised her head to look at me.

"After I got out of the army, I moved to Charleston. One of the guys from my unit owns a restaurant there."

Her face closed down. "Summer is in Charleston this weekend," she said. "At a food truck festival with her dad."

"I bet Alika is there. His restaurant has a food truck," I said. "That's actually how he met his wife."

Pressly scoffed. "Jeff is an asshole. He thinks I don't know he has a girlfriend in Charleston."

My jaw clenched. "You care that he has a girlfriend?"

Pressly laughed. "God, no. But I care that he isn't honest with me. He said he still loved me and he wanted me back, but then he has a side piece in Charleston."

"She's not a side piece if there is no main piece."

She relaxed into my arms. "You're right, of course. You've very smart."

"I do own a bookstore."

Several moments passed, and I thought she'd fallen asleep.

"Why didn't you ever get married? Start a family?" she asked.

My entire body stiffened, and not in a good way. I grabbed her hand and stilled her exploration of my chest. "I don't know."

She stared down at me, blue eyes bright on mine, refusing to let me off the hook. "Of course you do."

I closed my eyes, avoiding the probe of her gaze. "I never met the right woman," I said. "It was never the right time."

She pushed my hair off my forehead and dropped a kiss to my brow. "I'm glad. If you would have gotten married, you might not be here with me right now." She laughed softly. "Does that make me a selfish bitch?"

A low laugh vibrated in my chest, and I pulled her back down to the bed. "Yes, it does."

But I was selfish, too, because I was glad that prick Jeff had left her so she could move back to Mossy Oak. Maybe this was the reason I'd never shared my life with anyone. Maybe Pressly and I were meant to find each other again.

"I had an idea," she said. "About Fight Night."

We'd never officially ended our argument about the fight, and I knew we would circle back to it eventually. But it was after midnight, and I didn't really want to start the discussion, especially when I had to get up at 4:00 a.m. for a five-mile run. "Let's talk about it later, okay?" I yawned, pulling the sheet over us.

She snuggled against me, and a moment later, I felt the mattress sag as both Aslan and Daisy jumped onto the bed to join us.

* * *

Pressly was still asleep when I got back from my run. It was too early to wake her, so I poured a cup of coffee, fed the dogs, and wandered into Pete's office.

It was time to finish what I'd started. Pete wouldn't want me to leave his most treasured room unfinished. I sank onto the chair behind his desk, sipping my coffee as I gazed around the office. It would make a nice library.

There were already bookcases on both walls, which would save me some labor. I could update the desk, switch out the light fixture, and be done with it.

Which would mean I'd be done with the house. And then what?

My plan had been to put the house on the market, but now I wasn't so sure. I wasn't ready to quit being Pressly's neighbor.

Reaching into the bottom drawer, I pulled out the manilla envelope containing the letters to Pressly.

I wished I knew why Pete never delivered them to her, but unfortunately, he'd taken that information to his grave. I thought about reading the letters. I also thought about burning them. Nineteen-year-old Thatcher probably didn't have anything interesting to say.

"Hey, you got any more of that coffee?"

My head snapped up, and I saw Pressly standing in the doorway. She was wearing one of my T-shirts, and her makeup was smudged beneath her eyes. Her hair was messier than I'd ever seen it, probably from what we'd been up to all night in my bed. She looked adorable.

"Of course," I said, shoving the letters into the top drawer of Pete's desk. I stood and crossed the room, pulling her to me for a warm hug. "What are you doing this morning?" I asked.

She eased back and raised a brow. "Is that a trick question?"

I smoothed back her just-fucked hair. "Not at all."

A wicked smile curved her lips. "I'm spending it with you."

"Good." I turned her in the direction of the kitchen and smacked her on the ass. "You're coming with me to the gym."

She tossed her hair over her shoulder. "I can think of better ways to spend our time."

"We'll do that, too," I said. "But I have to train, and I want you with me."

"You're possessive," she said, arching a brow as I filled a mug with hot coffee.

"You like it."

She cocked her head at me, blue eyes glinting with a witchy gleam. "I think I do."

"I have a press conference later, but until then, you're stuck with me." I hated bringing up the press conference in case it started our argument where we'd left off, but Pressly let it drop.

An hour later, we were at the gym, and Pressly's first request was that I show her how to throw a proper punch.

"I'd say you have a pretty solid right already," I said, pinching the bridge of my nose, which still stung from her jab.

"That was a mistake," she said. "I need to know how to do it for real." The steely glint in her eyes told me she had a target in mind, and I didn't have to wonder if his last name was Carleton.

I showed her the proper stance and follow-through, taking full advantage of the situation to place my hands on her hips for guidance.

She was a natural.

By the time we were finished, sweat had beaded on her brow and stained her sports bra. I'd never been so hot for a sweaty woman in my life.

The gym was packed, and I noticed some of the regulars checking her out. Time to stake my claim.

I pulled her into my arms, pressing a kiss to her lips that left no doubt about who she was going home with.

"What's for lunch?" she asked.

I groaned. "Chicken and rice. Maybe some broccoli."

She shoved my chest playfully, then reached for her phone as Summer's ringtone sounded.

"Hey, sweetie," she said, smiling. "How's the festival?" Her face fell, and she pressed the phone to her ear, pushing out of my arms. "I can't hear you. What?"

Jay came up next to me as I watched Pressly pace across the gym floor.

"You fucking her?" he asked.

Something snapped inside me, and I turned on Jay. Even though he towered over me, I lunged at him, grabbing the front of his shirt.

"Don't talk about her like that."

Every eye in the gym turned to stare at us, but I ignored them, glaring at Jay. He held his arms up in an innocent gesture. "I'm just trying to look out for you," he said. "I don't trust her."

"It's none of your business."

His nostrils flared, and his jaw clenched. "Be cool. Keep your head on straight."

"I've got this," I said, raking a hand through my hair.

"Good." He crossed his arms over his chest. "I saw the proofs from the photo shoot. Not bad. Cassandra was thrilled."

My gaze drifted across the gym floor to Pressly. She met my gaze and frowned, shaking her head. Something was wrong.

Thirty

Thatcher strode across the gym. "What happened?"

I dragged in a deep breath, trying to keep calm. "Summer is lost," I said. I swiped to Jeff's number and pressed Call. "That sorry son of a bitch better answer his phone," I muttered, waiting while Jeff's phone rang and then went to voicemail. "Pick up the fucking phone, Jeff!"

Thatcher's hands closed over my shoulders. "What's going on?"

I gestured for him to wait while I spoke into the phone in a menacing voice. "Jeff, call me back as soon as possible." I hung up and pulled in another shaky breath before looking up at Thatcher. "Summer is lost at the festival in Charleston. She can't find Jeff, and she's hysterical. I need to call her back." I swiped my finger over my phone to call her, then stopped, feeling helpless. I was so far away. There was nothing I could do. "This is all my fault."

"It's not your fault," Thatcher said. "This is on Jeff." He lifted my chin so that our eyes met. "It's gonna be okay. Call her back and talk to her. I think I can help."

While he grabbed his phone from his duffel bag, I called Summer back. I could hear the tears in her voice when she answered, and it broke my heart. "Hey, baby," I said. "Everything is okay."

"What do I do, Mommy? I'm scared."

A lump formed in my throat to hear her call me Mommy. It had been years since she'd called me anything but Mom.

I didn't know what to do other than keep her talking until Jeff called me back. "Tell me where you are," I said. "What do you see?"

She sniffed loudly. "There are people everywhere. And animals. And trucks with food. And—"

Thatcher stalked across the gym. "Let me talk to her," he said.

"Summer, Thatcher wants to talk to you for a minute. Don't hang up when you're done. I'll be waiting." My heart in my throat, I handed Thatcher the phone.

He gave me a reassuring smile and reached for my hand. "Hey, Winter. You okay?" His gaze held mine as he waited for her to answer. "Have you seen a statue of a man on a horse?" He nodded. "Okay, that's great. Head toward the statue."

Pulling me into his arms, he guided me out of the gym into the parking lot, away from the prying eyes. I leaned into him, letting my head rest against his solid shoulder. He stroked a hand over my hair, all the while directing Summer over the phone.

"Do you see a truck painted with Hawaiian flowers that says Ono Grinds?" he asked. His face brightened. "Good job!" He smiled down at me, his eyes bright. "There's a man standing in front of the truck. He's really big, like a refrigerator, but I promise he isn't scary. He's my best friend, and his name is Alika."

Thatcher handed the phone back to me.

"Summer? You're safe now. Stay with Thatcher's friend. I'm coming to get you."

After a tearful goodbye, I hung up, threw my arms around Thatcher's neck, and cried. He held me, rubbing his hand up and down my back, murmuring reassuring words.

"I need to go," I said.

"I'm coming with you."

"No," I said. "You have your press conference."

"Fuck the press conference. I don't want you going to Charleston by yourself. Plus, I want to be there when you see Jeff." He grinned. "I've got to see that right in action."

He mimed a punch, attempting to keep things light.

My phone rang, and my face heated when I saw Jeff's name light up my screen. I held my phone up so Thatcher could see it, and a thunderstorm crossed his expression. Tamping down the impatient roar of anger flooding my body, I answered.

"Pressly! Thank God you finally answered. I've been trying to call you."

My blood boiled, rushing through my ears. I couldn't believe the lies coming out of his mouth.

"Where are you, Jeff?" I asked, my voice miraculously calm.

"I'm at the festival, near Marion Square. Summer just disappeared. I took my eyes off her for one second, and she was gone."

"She's safe now," I said.

"Where?"

If I didn't know better, I'd think he was actually a concerned dad. "She's with a friend," I said.

"Listen, Pressly." He lowered his voice. "It wasn't my fault. She ran off."

I rolled my eyes. "I thought you took your eyes off her."

"Whatever." He sucked wind. "Tell me where she is."

I glanced up at Thatcher. He was watching me with fierce determination, ready to swoop in if I needed him. I reached for his hand, and he squeezed my fingers so hard it was almost too much. Somehow, it was perfect.

"Jeff, I'm gonna need to get back to you on that." I hung up on his sputtering response and called Summer. "Hey, sweetie. Are you still okay?"

"I'm good. CeeCee gave me a cinnamon roll, and Alika is really funny." She giggled. "He looks like a giant, but he's really nice."

My gaze found Thatcher's, and I mouthed, "Thank you."

He nodded once, a small smile lifting his lips.

"I just talked to your dad," I told Summer.

Her response was immediate. "He doesn't care about me. He's got Jennifer and her kids now, and they can ski."

My brows pulled together as I tried to piece together the information. Jennifer must be the girlfriend. "Okay. But he's your dad, and he's looking for you. Stay put, and I'll tell him where to find you."

"Do I have to?" she whined. "I don't want to go with him."

I didn't want her to go with Jeff either, but after surviving the messy divorce and custody battle, I knew it was better for Summer to comply. "I'm going to tell your dad where to find you, but then you can decide if you want to go with him or stay with Thatcher's friends."

"I want to stay with Thatcher's friends," she said. "And I want to go home."

I choked back tears. It was the first time I remembered Summer calling Mossy Oak home. "I'm coming for you."

When we hung up, I texted Jeff where to find Summer and informed him she wasn't going with him.

Thatcher handed me into his Jeep, and I sat with my head in my hands, catching my breath.

"I'll be right back." He jogged to the gym, coming back a moment later with his bag and a sports drink for me. "Drink this."

My hands shook as I lifted the cold bottle to my lips. I took a long sip, letting the cool sweet drink slide down my parched throat. "Thank you."

"No need," he said, shooting me a smile as he started the Jeep. "I've got your six."

"My what?"

He pulled out of the lot and headed home. "It just means I'm looking out for you."

I closed my eyes briefly, willing the dizziness to abate before I pulled out my phone and started researching flights to Charleston. There was one leaving in a few hours, but the return flight wasn't until the next day. I could rent a car and drive home tonight.

I groaned and rubbed my forehead. The logistics were giving me a headache.

Fucking Jeff.

I'd never wanted to punch him more in my life.

Thirty-One

It was late afternoon by the time I pulled into Alika's neighborhood in Charleston.

My daughter was in the hands of a stranger, but he was Thatcher's friend. Despite how Thatcher had let me down in the past, I trusted him.

He'd tried to insist on coming with me, but I'd refused to let him. It was important to me that I handled the situation on my own.

I found a place to park on the crowded street in front of the colorful row houses. Charleston had always been one of my favorite cities, but now it was tainted because of Jeff.

I checked the address again and walked up to the tall house painted a cheerful yellow. A woman answered the door, and music spilled out onto the street.

She was slightly out of breath, sweat beading on her brow, and her smile was like a ray of sunshine.

"You must be Summer's mama." She reached for my hand and drew me inside. "She looks exactly like you."

My heart pounded in my chest, and I glanced into the house, searching for a sign of my daughter. "Is she okay?"

The woman squeezed my hand. "Bless your heart. You've

been dragged through the mud today, haven't you?" She gestured toward the source of the music. "We're having a little dance party."

I was suddenly fifty pounds lighter as the weight lifted from my shoulders. "Thank you."

"No problem." She smiled warmly. "I'm CeeCee."

"Pressly."

"You have a very special little girl," CeeCee said. "She's fabulous with Leo." CeeCee led me through the house to a screened-in porch where music was blasting.

I saw Summer dancing with a little boy who looked like he belonged in a Disney movie. He was about three years old, with chubby cheeks and a headful of dark, springy curls. His smile showed a mouthful of tiny white teeth, and his giggle sent a rush of warmth through me. But it was Summer who made my breath catch.

She was laughing with Leo, spinning in circles that made her hair fly around her face. My little girl was so beautiful, but more importantly, she was safe.

Jeff, on the other hand, was dead meat.

"Summer!" CeeCee called. "Your mama's here."

Summer came to a halt mid-spin and ran across the room. She threw her arms around my waist and held on for dear life. I was so shocked I almost fell over. I couldn't remember the last time Summer had voluntarily touched me.

"Hey, Summer." I hugged her close, my heart melting. "I'm so glad to see you."

"I was so scared, Mom," she said, pushing her head into my chest.

"It's okay." We held on to each other until I wasn't sure who was supporting whom. "You're safe now."

Leo rushed over and wrapped his arms around both of our legs, clinging tightly. Summer giggled and reached down to include him in the hug. It tore at my heart to see her with the little boy. I'd always wanted another child, but Jeff had put me off, saying one was enough.

I pulled back and forced a smile. "You ready to get home? Aslan missed you."

"Have something to eat first. Eh?" A deep voice boomed through the room.

I turned around and saw an intimidating hulk of a man looming in the doorway. He had close-cropped black hair, perfect bone structure, and shoulders the size of mountains. Swirling lines of ink peeked out from under the sleeves of his T-shirt.

"Alika's always trying to feed everyone," CeeCee said, slipping her arm around her husband's waist.

"I wouldn't want to put you out any more than we already have," I said.

"It's no problem," Alika said. "Any friend of Thatcher's is a friend of ours." The corner of his mouth tipped up in a grin. "And I'm an amazing cook. It would be a shame to miss out."

"Shut up," CeeCee said, poking Alika in the ribs. "If your ego gets any bigger, you won't be able to fit through the kitchen door."

Alika's dark brows pulled together, but he didn't argue. "Eat," he said. "Then you can hit the road with a full belly."

"No!" Leo protested, holding on to Summer's leg. "I want to keep her."

Alika strode forward and plucked the little boy into his arms. "We can't keep her, buddy," he said. "But maybe she can come visit again soon."

"Can we stay a little longer, Mom?" Summer asked.

I glanced around the room at the expectant faces. Getting home was my first priority, but my stomach growled at the idea of a meal. "Are you sure it's okay?"

CeeCee smiled. "Of course. We always have too much food. This one can't stop cooking. It's a wonder I don't weigh three hundred pounds."

Alika's eyes roamed over his wife, and his mouth tipped up in a smile. "You'd look cute with a little more meat on your bones."

"You're impossible," she said, returning his smile.

It was obvious from the way they looked at each other that they were madly in love. Envy flared, burning in my chest. I'd married Jeff with the expectation that it would last forever, but it hadn't worked out that way.

We took seats in the kitchen at a small round table and passed around containers of food. Alika encouraged me to take a sample of everything, explaining he was developing a new recipe and wanted my opinion.

It was impossible to choose a favorite because everything was so delicious. There were spring rolls filled with vegetables, dumplings, and something he called Spam musubi, which was actually made from Spam.

The seasoned rice and pulled chicken made me think of Thatcher, and for a moment, I wished I'd allowed him to come with me.

"I can't eat another bite," I said when Alika pushed a plate of coconut pudding toward me.

"Come on," he said. "You have to try."

I groaned in protest but eventually relented. When I was more stuffed than a Thanksgiving turkey, I pushed my plate away. "Enough."

CeeCee laughed and stood up to clear the table. When I insisted on helping, she wouldn't hear of it. "How about a cup of coffee before you hit the road?"

I was feeling drowsy from overeating and nodded. "I would appreciate it."

"How's my man Thatcher doing?" Alika asked.

"He's the best," Summer said before I could answer.

Alika met my eyes over Summer's head, and I managed a small nod. "He's great."

"Is he now?" CeeCee asked, lifting an eyebrow.

Alika gave his wife a look, and she shrugged. "What? I want to hear all about how awesome Thatcher is." Her gaze slid to me, curious eyes shining.

My cheeks flushed just thinking of Thatcher, and CeeCee grinned, seeming to read my mind.

"He makes the best displays at the bookstore," Summer said. "They look like something from a movie set."

"Book!" Leo cried and scurried off on his chubby legs. He came back a moment later with a picture book and thrust it at Summer. "Book!"

"Summer, will you read to him while your mom has a cup of coffee?" CeeCee asked.

Summer's face brightened, and she took the book from Leo. "Sure."

"He likes to sit in the rocking chair," Alika said, pointing toward the living room.

At the mention of his favorite chair, Leo tugged Summer into the other room.

"Back to Thatcher," CeeCee said, wiggling her brows.

"CeeCee," Alika growled. "Don't."

She leveled him with an innocent stare. "What? I'm thinking about getting some displays for the truck."

He grabbed her around the waist and spun her into his arms. "You better not be."

She giggled as he lifted her off her feet. They were the cutest couple I'd ever seen. Even though they were sweet, I couldn't help feeling envious of their connection.

"How do you know Thatcher?" I asked.

"He didn't say?" Alika asked, his eyes searching mine.

I searched my memory, but I'd been half-asleep and very satisfied when we'd been discussing his Charleston friend. "He mentioned moving here after he got out of the army."

Alika crossed the room and grabbed a framed photo from a shelf. "Here we are," he said. "A couple of dumb kids."

I took the picture and saw three young men with freshly buzzed hair dressed in army uniforms. Thatcher looked just like he had the summer we first met, minus the long, flowing locks. And Alika looked like a fresh-faced boy. I didn't recognize the other man.

"When was this?" I asked, staring at the photo.

"Right after we enlisted," Alika said. "September of 2001." He shook his head, a sad smile tugging at his lips. "We thought we were gonna save the world from terrorists, but it didn't work out that way."

Confusion made my head pound. "September 2001?" I asked. Thatcher and I had met in June of 2001, so that couldn't be right. "But Thatcher was in college."

"Nope." Alika took the photo from me and studied the three stern-faced young men with their shorn heads. "After Thatcher's dad died during the attacks on 9/11, he dropped out of school and joined the army." A bark of laughter escaped his mouth. "At least he had a good reason. I was just a dumbass."

CeeCee slipped her arms around Alika's waist from behind. "You were heroes," she said.

He turned, and his arms went around her. He rested his chin on the top of her head and dropped a kiss on her hair. "Thanks, babe."

Alika's words sank in, and I felt like a fool. Thatcher hadn't stood me up because he didn't want me. I'd spent years being angry at him for nothing.

And worse, I'd wasted all that time avoiding him when we could have been together.

Thirty-Two

Logan "The Hitman" Malone stood across from me with his fists raised, teeth bared, and muscles bulging.

I could see why the fans loved him.

He was a true showman.

Tattoos snaked up his neck and into the shaved portion of his scalp, and his cocky attitude announced him coming from across the room.

"I'm gonna fuck you up, Pretty Boy." He sneered at me, shifting the toothpick in his mouth from one side to the other. "But maybe you like getting fucked?" His hips rocked in an unmistakable rhythm, and he winked at me.

I plucked the toothpick from his mouth and flicked it across the room. "I do like getting fucked," I said, picturing the woman who'd made me come not too long ago spread out on my king-sized mattress. "Too bad all you have is your hand."

Nothing Logan said could bother me. I was on top of the world. Pressly might have stood me up all those years ago, but she was mine now. We were together, and it was even better than I'd ever imagined.

Logan pushed his chest into me, knocking me off-balance.

"How about a side bet?" he asked. "I win and you shave off all that pretty hair."

Despite what people thought, I wasn't vain about my hair. I'd worn it buzzed while I was in the army, and I kept it long more out of neglect than style.

"And if I win, you get a tattoo of Tweety Bird," I said, figuring it wasn't too big of an ask, considering he already had ink covering half his body.

"Deal." He extended his hand to me, turning slightly to the cameras for the photo opportunity.

The cameras flashed, and then we were done. I was anxious to get back to training, and once the cameras were gone, Malone was gone. He didn't give a fuck about me unless someone was filming. He was so confident he was going to beat me I wasn't even on his radar.

Cassandra pulled me aside when the room emptied. She was so tall in her high heels we were at eye level. "That was great," she said, hyping me up. "You really got in his head."

I snorted on a laugh. "You think so?"

"I know so. He's going to have to find room for that tattoo come Saturday."

I nodded, my mind already on the long training session ahead.

Jay was waiting for me at the gym. Only a few more days before I had to prove myself in the ring. I had six more pounds to lose before weigh-in, but there was no way I wasn't making it.

"One-two-three, one-two-three," Jay called as I hit the punching bag. "You gotta be faster than that if you want to take him." Jay circled the bag, scowling. "Keep your hands up. If you let him get a lucky punch, you're done."

The way I saw it, there was no such thing as a lucky punch. That's what training was for—being prepared. If Malone was banking on a lucky punch, he'd better think again.

When I was done on the bag, Dumptruck was waiting for me in the ring to spar. At seventeen years old, the up-and-coming junior boxer was large and square—hence his nickname. He was making his debut on Fight Night, and most of the kids from Champion's Corner were at the gym to watch him train.

"Bring it on, old man," he said, sneering around his mouthpiece.

I hated to humiliate a kid, but I couldn't hold myself back. We exchanged a flurry of punches, the session ending with mutual respect.

When I was finally finished for the day, I hit the steam room, where I hoped to sweat off a few more pounds. Closing my eyes, I rested my head against the wall and tried to relax.

The door to the steam room opened and closed, but I didn't bother to look up. I was just too tired.

"Thatcher."

Either my ears were deceiving me, or there was an angel in the room. I opened my eyes, and through the layers of steam, I could see her silhouette: Pressly.

She crossed the room, coming out of the mist. A smile spread over her lips as her eyes dropped over me. "Nice towel."

I was wearing one of the tiny towels Jay provided the clients of Out of the Box. Cheap motherfucker—he couldn't even order full-sized towels.

Pressly's hungry gaze made me thankful for Jay's thriftiness. I was suddenly very awake.

Pressly's gaze drifted over me, and I knew she liked what she saw. I was in the best shape of my life. Every muscle in my torso was lean and defined, and the tiny towel did little to hide her effect on me.

"It's crazy hot in here." She fanned herself, but she was looking at me. At my lower half, in particular.

"You walking in here just upped the temperature a hundred degrees." I smiled, wanting nothing more than to eat her up, too. Hopefully, we'd get to that later. But first, there was her little girl. "Is everything okay with Summer?"

She nodded. "She's in there with the rest of the club, celebrating. Apparently, Dumptruck kicked your ass?"

I scoffed. "Is that right?"

She stepped closer, and I sat up, spreading my legs so she could stand between them.

"Thank you," she said. "For everything."

"You're welcome."

She linked her arms around my neck and lowered her mouth to mine. The kiss was soft, just a brush of her mouth, promising more to come. "I really appreciate you."

I wrapped her in my arms. "I appreciate you, too."

"I think I'm melting," Pressly said. "I don't know how you stand it in here."

I laughed. "Lots of practice. And I needed it. Every muscle in my body aches after what Jay put me through today."

One of her perfect eyebrows lifted. "I know it's been a crazy day, but I told Summer she could watch a movie with the rest of the kids tonight. She needs to do something normal." Pressly's mouth curved in a smile. "And they invited her."

I knew it was a big deal for Summer to have a group of friends.

Pressly sifted her hands through my damp hair, fingers massaging my scalp. "Maybe you need a massage. I could come over for a little while before she gets dropped off."

I sighed and rested my head on her shoulder as her hands worked magic on my aching neck. "Are you sure? It's been a long day."

She tugged my head back, covering my mouth with a hot kiss. "Absolutely."

I stood and pulled her into my arms, almost losing the towel. If we didn't get out of the steam room soon, it was going to get indecent.

"I'll meet you at my place," I said. "The back door's unlocked."

She slipped out of my arms and brushed by me into the hall. "See you there."

When I got home, the lights blazed downstairs, and I knew Pressly was waiting for me. It was something I could get used to.

"Do you want wine?" I asked, tossing my keys on the counter and heading toward the pantry. "I've got a bottle of red in here somewhere."

I couldn't have any, but I could watch her drink and taste the rich flavor on her lips.

Daisy came to greet me, and I filled her water bowl at the sink before setting it down and moving through the living room.

"Pressly?" I asked, heading toward the stairs, hoping she was waiting for me in bed, naked.

"In here," she called.

I froze at the sound of her voice coming from Pete's office.

Thirty-Three

I held the envelope with my name written on it out to Thatcher. "What is this?"

His entire demeanor changed, going rigid. "What are you doing in here?"

"I was looking for a piece of paper," I said.

He strode forward and took the envelope out of my hands. "I was gonna give these to you," he said, sounding like I'd just ripped his heart from his chest.

"When?" I stared down at the bulging envelope.

He reached for me, but I took a step back. His gaze clashed with mine. "I don't know."

"What's in there that you don't want me to see?"

"Just some dumb letters. Pete was supposed to give them to you." He smiled, but it rang false. "Guess I'm glad he didn't. Some pretty embarrassing shit, I'm sure."

"Letters?" I asked. "You wrote me letters?"

His tongue pushed into his cheek, and he nodded. "From war."

"CeeCee said you were a hero."

His gaze sliced to mine, and he bit out a humorless laugh. "Fuck that."

The haunted look in his eyes chilled me to the bone. "You had a good reason for not meeting me that night." I stepped closer to him, feeling the vulnerability pulsing off him in waves. "All these years, I thought you didn't care about me enough to meet me. I was wrong."

His gaze sharpened. "I thought you didn't show up either."

I straightened my shoulders, refusing to be ashamed for protecting myself. "I lied," I said.

His eyes narrowed, and his jaw clenched. "You lied about not coming to meet me?"

I nodded. "I was there, Thatcher." My throat closed, but I forced the words out. "I waited for hours, hoping you would come." A shiver passed over me as I remembered that chilly night in November, waiting for the love of my life to show up. "I wish I would have known what happened to you. Why you didn't show up."

The color drained from his face. "You showed up?"

"I did."

He dropped the envelope and gathered me against his chest, where his warmth surrounded me. "I'm so sorry."

His grip was so tight I could hardly breathe, and I knew this was about more than the lie I'd told. This was about whatever had happened in Africa that made panic descend on him in the most inopportune moments.

I stroked a hand over the trembling muscles in his back. Seeing him broken was even worse than seeing him frozen after I'd accidentally punched him.

"It's okay," I said. "It was so long ago."

"I broke your heart."

I buried my face in his chest. "You were the first." He was the first everything. My first crush. My first lover. My first disappointment. "But it was only because I loved you."

"Shit." He suddenly pushed me away, raking a hand through his hair. "Things could have been so different." He glanced down at the envelope. "I thought you read those and didn't care."

I watched his face close down and knew he was thinking about something other than the missed opportunity for us.

"What happened over there?" I asked.

His lips flattened. "I don't talk about it."

I put my hand on his shoulder, feeling the tension ripple through him. "Maybe you should."

He laughed bitterly. "I've had therapy before," he said. "It doesn't work."

My fingers trailed down his arm. "What does work?"

He shook his head. "Boxing used to. Until it didn't."

Frustration burned in my chest. "But you're doing it anyway. You're gonna risk your life in that ring, for what?"

"I have to," he insisted.

"No. You don't." I leaned against the desk, suddenly worn out from the long day. "What if there was a donation to the gym? Wouldn't that solve the problem?"

He crossed his arms over his chest. "A donation is nice," he said. "But it's a bandage. Out of the Box has a reputation to uphold. If there's no Fight Night, there's no credibility."

"I don't see how you can fight," I said.

"I don't see how I can't."

My heart felt like it was going to burst through my chest. "Well, I can't watch it."

He looked down at the floor for a long moment, then raised his gaze to me. There was a cold look in his eyes I'd never seen before. "No big deal, babe." He shrugged. "It's up to you."

"So you don't care if I'm there?"

He shook his head, not quite meeting my eyes. "As long as I can see you after."

I glanced down at the envelope on the floor, dying for Thatcher to pick it up and hand it to me. I wouldn't take it otherwise, even if it was addressed to me. Those were his letters, not mine.

When he made no move to retrieve them, I sighed heavily and turned toward the door. "I should go. It's been a long day."

"Hey," he said, snagging my hand, pulling me back into the office. "Remember what you promised."

I allowed him to tug me into his arms, and then the next thing I knew, we were kissing. Softly at first, a tentative meeting of our mouths. We were both emotionally wrung out, and it felt good to find comfort in each other.

Then the tension of the day slowly melted away, and the kiss became more urgent. His tongue sought mine, stroking and teasing. I opened for him, sliding my hands over his hard body, pressing my hips against his.

When I hooked my leg around him, his hand slid under my knee and glided up my leg until he gripped my ass. His hard erection pressed into me, and something broke inside me.

I felt wild.

The kiss became frenzied, a clash of mouths, teeth, and tongues. I couldn't get enough of his taste, his scent, his feel.

Electricity zinged between us as we kissed hard, fumbling with our clothes. He tore my blouse open, covering my chest with hot, wet kisses.

He pulled his shirt over his head as I shrugged out of my blouse. Unhooking my bra, he slid it off me and filled his hands with my breasts.

I arched into him on a long moan. I could never get enough of him. He nipped and sucked, leaving angry marks with his teeth that he soothed with his hot tongue.

Reaching for his pants, I undid his zipper and freed his throbbing cock into my hand. Stroking roughly, I made him so hard he felt like velvet-wrapped steel.

We didn't have to tell each other what we wanted. We didn't say a word as we stripped off the rest of our clothes.

He used two fingers under my chin to raise my face. When our eyes connected, I felt my world slide. Everything I'd once hoped and dreamed for was reflected in his gaze. Once again, I was the young girl with the world at her feet. I was the girl who dared to ask for what she wanted and was brave enough to take it when it was offered.

I threaded my fingers through his hair and guided his mouth to mine. We kissed again, and something felt different. The urgency was gone, replaced by something intensely powerful.

I'd been through hell in the last few years, and Thatcher felt like a reward for my suffering.

A tall, sculpted, well-endowed reward.

I shifted forward so we were lined up and wrapped my arms around his neck. Our eyes met, and I felt the intensity of his stare all the way to my toes. He kissed me again, taking my mouth with a gentleness I remembered all too well from years of replaying our summer together in my mind. Slowly, he guided himself inside me.

I gasped as he filled me, and clung to his shoulders. Tension radiated off his back, and his muscles tensed as he rolled his hips.

Pleasure thundered through me, and every muscle in my body tightened.

"Fuck," Thatcher moaned against my mouth.

The vibration of his words rumbled through me even as he rocked inside me.

A tear slid down my cheek, and the salty wetness tainted our kiss.

"Hey." Thatcher pulled back, his gorgeous blue eyes filled with worry. "Are you okay? Did I hurt you?"

Unable to choke out any words, I clung to him, angling my body in a way that made all my thoughts fade away. I ground against him, and the sensations of pleasure overtook my emotions.

His hands gripped my hips, pulling me impossibly closer until there was no way to tell where one of us ended and the other began. I should have known letting Thatcher into my life would feel like splitting myself wide open. I'd known him so briefly and so long ago, but he had the ability to destroy me. To make me want things I'd given up on having.

With a low moan that sent a tingle down my spine, he drove into me, filling me again and again. His hands gripped my hips, and his mouth claimed mine.

There wasn't an inch of me that didn't belong to him.

For the moment, there were no lies, no letters from war, no upcoming fight.

There was only us.

June 2002

Dear Peppy,

The past few days have been rough. Killing is everywhere. Capturing and burning villages is a way of life. Some of the child soldiers are so small they can barely carry their weapons.

These child soldiers are so high on drugs and violence, they think they are immune to death.

They are convinced we are the enemy when we are only here to save them.

We have no idea what they've gone through. They see our brand-new guns that have never been fired and don't think we are real soldiers.

They laugh at us for tucking our shirts into our pants and our pants into our boots and wait for an opportunity to steal our weapons.

They were told they were fighting for their villages, for their freedom, but it was all a lie. This country is crawling with liars and murderers.

I think about the boys I coached this summer and it seems like a different life.

I miss you.

You're the only person in my life who tried to get to know me. Who really listened.

Remember how we stayed up all night talking, telling each other our plans for life? I hope yours are working out better than mine.

I should have told you I loved you in person when I had the chance.

Sincerely, Thatcher Hayes

P.S. This is a picture of me and my best friends, Alika and John. I hope you will get to meet them someday.

Thirty-Four

Placing one foot in front of the other, I pounded the pavement, trying to focus on my stride instead of the tangle of thoughts in my head.

I hated running.

Not the physical aspect of it. I could handle the cardio and endurance. I could run for miles, but I could never escape my thoughts.

And running gave my mind the perfect opportunity to drift to unpleasant places.

Like those fucking letters.

I couldn't remember what I'd written, but it was sure to be embarrassing and worse—incriminating.

My steps faltered, and I stopped for a second to drag in a breath. I'd written everything in those letters, poured my stupid heart out.

I'd written about Josiah. And the rehabilitation center. And... fuck.

I started running again. One foot in front of the other.

Don't think about the letters. Don't think about Josiah. Don't think about blood dripping from the trees or the smell of burning flesh.

I picked up the pace, sprinting even though Jay had strictly forbidden it. Running was supposed to be for endurance, not strength.

But I couldn't help it. I needed to race, to leave my thoughts behind.

I sprinted all the way back to Sweet Gum Lane, then forced myself to slow down as I neared my house. My heart thundered, and my legs were on fire.

And those letters were gonna be right where I left them.

I dragged my feet as I approached my house, dreading walking by the office and seeing them on the floor.

As I trudged up the steps to my house, Beckett's car pulled into Pressly's driveway.

"Hey, Mr. T!" Summer called as she hopped out of the car.

Aslan bounded down beside her, then ran over to greet me. I crouched and rubbed his ears. "Hey, buddy."

When I stood up, Beckett was looming over me. When we'd first met, he'd been a skinny kid with thick glasses. Now he wasn't so skinny, and he towered over me. The only thing that hadn't changed was the glasses.

"Thanks for your help in Charleston," he said, shaking my hand.

"Pressly told you about that?"

He nodded, a scowl settling over his features. "I wished I could have been there to help. But I'm glad she's got you. Thanks, man."

My chest swelled. I'd never met Pressly's dad, but Beckett's approval was good enough for me. "You're welcome."

"I could kill Jeff," he said.

"Get in line." I glanced over his shoulder and saw Summer coming across the lawn. "I'd do anything for her," I said.

Beckett's brows raised above the dark frames of his glasses. "Pressly or Summer?"

I shrugged, meeting his gaze. "Both."

"Guess what, Mr. T!"

I shifted and looked at Summer. She was adorable in a "Cats of Obsidian" T-shirt and a puffy cheetah-print skirt. "You lost something?" I asked, pointing to her missing tooth.

She clapped her hand over her mouth and giggled. "No! I got my nickname!"

All the kids earned nicknames at Champion's Corner. "Cool," I said. "What did you pick?"

She smiled proudly. "Storm."

"Nice."

"Thanks," Summer said. "It goes with Summer and Winter."

"Ah." My heart squeezed. Little squirt wanted to keep my nickname for her.

"You coming to Fight Night?" I asked.

"Yeah," she said, looking at me like I was crazy for asking. "Everyone from Champion's Corner will be there. Iceman is making her debut."

"She's gonna do great."

"Maybe someday I can fight," Summer said.

"Maybe." Beckett and I exchanged a look. We both knew it wasn't likely Pressly would let her fight in a match.

"Iceman is doing it," she said, reading our exchanged glance.

"We'll see, kiddo," Beckett said, patting her shoulder. "First, we need to fuel up. Pizza or fried chicken?"

"Pizza!"

Summer was a girl after my own heart. I'd been craving pizza for weeks.

Beckett grinned. "Bet it sucks eating all that healthy chicken and rice."

I flipped him the bird behind Summer's back.

His grin widened. "It's worth it, though. Stronger and quicker, remember?"

I nodded. "Yeah, sure, but I really want pizza. And beer."

Beckett laughed. "Go on inside and feed Aslan," he told Summer. "He's probably starving."

When Summer was gone, Beckett pinned me with a probing gaze. "How are you feeling otherwise?"

I knew what he was asking. Jay had shared with Beckett about my last fight when I'd frozen up, and Beckett had strategized ways to prevent it from happening again. He'd sent me links to dozens of videos, and I'd dutifully watched them all.

But I'd never really know until I got in the ring.

"Rock solid," I said, tapping a fist to my chest.

"You got this," he said.

"I know."

My confidence drained as soon as I walked by Pete's office and spied the envelope with the letters just inside the door where Pressly and I had dropped them.

Just looking at them caused anxiety to ripple through me. My therapist would call me out on this, say I needed to deal with my shit instead of blowing it up in my mind.

I grabbed my phone and called Pressly.

"Hello?"

Just hearing her voice made me smile. "Hey. Where are you?"

"At work," she said, laughing softly. "Where are you?"

"I just got done with a run."

"Ugh. I hate running."

"Me too." I walked by the office and stared at the envelope on the floor.

"Are you sore? I could give you another massage."

My blood warmed, pumping faster. "I don't remember us ever getting to that massage the other night."

"I'll have to make it up to you."

I stared at the letters, and silence stretched across the line as I tried to think of what to say.

"Thatcher?"

"Yeah?"

"I should go," she said. "It's crazy here right now. I'll talk to you later?"

"Yeah, sure."

"Everything okay?"

"It's fine, we'll talk later."

With one final look at the envelope, I headed up the stairs, vowing not to think about the letters until after the fight. I wouldn't even walk by Pete's office again until the fight was over.

A long, hot shower would make me feel better, and maybe I'd take Pressly up on that massage later.

There was a knock on the door when I was almost to the top of the stairs. "It's open," I called.

Summer poked her head inside. "Hi!"

"Hello. What's up?"

"I was wondering if I could borrow a cup of dog food? We ran out, and Aslan is still hungry."

"Sure." I continued up the stairs. "You know where Daisy's food is. Help yourself."

"You should lock your door," Summer said. "Especially if you're getting in the bath."

"What makes you think I'm getting in the bath?" I asked, watching her until she disappeared down the hall.

"You smell pretty bad," she said from the kitchen.

"Lock the door on your way out," I yelled, laughing as I went into my bathroom. Kid was right—I reeked. But I was smiling. And it felt damn good.

Thirty-Five

My stomach growled, but I ignored it. I didn't have time to eat. There were too many phone calls to return, too many spreadsheets to consult, and I still needed to make my a.m. rounds before noon. I stared at my monitor, watching all the numbers squish together as my vision blurred. Maybe it was time to get my eyes checked. Eye disease ran in our family.

I took a deep breath, trying to push away the worries that nagged my mind. But it was no use. I had already stumbled into the worry zone.

A knock sounded at my door, and a moment later, it opened. Beckett darted inside and slammed the door behind him.

"I had to sneak past Chef Gio." He hurried over to my desk and plopped down a takeout bag. "That man is unhinged."

My mouth watered at the sight of the logo for Tripp's Fried Chicken, my absolute favorite guilty pleasure. "Gio's just passionate," I said in defense of the best chef Sky Valley Resort had ever known. "What are you doing here?" I asked. "I thought you were in New York."

"Not this week," he said. "The fight's in two days."

At the mention of Thatcher's fight, my appetite plummeted.

Beckett pulled a Styrofoam cup from the holder and handed it to me. "Tea okay?"

I pushed the image of Thatcher bloodied and broken to the far corner of my mind and stabbed the straw through the lid. I took a long sip of perfectly sweetened iced tea and smiled faintly. No one made sweet tea like Tripp.

Beckett opened the paper bag. The smell of fried chicken wafted into the room, and I had to restrain myself from diving for the container.

"There better be seasoned fries in there," I said.

"Who do you think you're talking to? Of course there are seasoned fries."

Beckett took out two containers and handed me one. I flipped the lid open and inhaled the smell of greasy fried chicken and french fries. Sinking my teeth into a crispy, salted fry, I eyed Beckett. "You remember Aunt Francine?" I asked.

He cocked his head at me. "The blind old bat with the receding hairline?"

"Yeah."

"Why?"

"Blindness runs in the family."

Taking a bite of chicken, he mumbled around the mouthful. "You're going crazy."

"I am not."

"Aunt Francine wasn't even in our family," he said. "She was adopted."

"What?"

"You knew that."

"No, I didn't."

"Her family died when she was young. Gran took her in, raised her as her own. She said she figured one more wouldn't hurt because there were already seven of them."

I put down my chicken and gazed at the wall behind Beckett's head, feeling like the rug had been pulled out from under my feet.

"I don't know what's true anymore," I said.

Beckett laughed. "You're definitely losing it," he said. "You do know it isn't February."

"Of course." A dull ache settled in my chest when I thought of Thatcher. Things had been a little off since that night I'd found the letters in his office. But he hadn't mentioned them again, and if he wanted me to have them, he would have given them to me.

"It's April 26," he said.

"I know what day it is, Beckett."

"So why is your calendar on February?" He nodded his chin behind me.

"I forgot to change it," I said.

"For two months?"

I got up and pulled the calendar from the wall. "I never even look at that," I said. "I use the calendar on my laptop."

Beckett snagged one of my fries and shoved it in his mouth. "What's going on with the two of you?"

He reached for another fry, and I smacked his hand. "Eat your own fries," I said.

"Already did."

It was time to get rid of my baby brother before he started asking more questions. "Here," I said, pushing the container of fries at him. "Take them with you."

He raised an eyebrow at me as he munched another fry. "Are you kicking me out?"

I wiped my hands on a napkin and reached into my drawer for my notebook. "I really appreciate lunch, but I need to get back to work. My boss is a real jerk."

Beckett grinned because as CEO of Vinroot Enterprises, technically, *he* was my boss. He helped himself to another french fry. "Answer the question."

"What question?"

"Don't play dumb."

"I'm not. I have no idea what you're talking about." I grabbed a pen from the holder on my desk. "If you'll excuse me, I need to make my rounds."

Beckett leaned back in his chair, eyeing me with a teasing glint. "You're still carrying a torch for him. Admit it."

"Carrying a torch?" I laughed. "You're the one who's losing your mind."

"You've been in love with Thatcher since you were seventeen." Beckett got up and walked around to my desk to retrieve the calendar from the trash can. He flipped it open to February and held it up to face me. "This probably has drool on it," he said, grimacing.

Heat filled my cheeks. "You're so juvenile." I tried to grab the calendar from him, but he waved it over his head out of reach. I punched him, and he winced, faking injury.

"Ouch," he whined, grabbing his stomach. "Here, take it."

When I reached for the calendar, he yanked it away at the last second and smacked me on the head with it.

"You messed up my hair," I said, straightening my updo.

Beckett laughed. "Relax," he said. "You could use a little messing up. The employees are complaining about the manager being too uptight."

My jaw dropped. "I'm not uptight."

Crossing his arms over his chest, he let his gaze drop over my outfit. "Your turtleneck is cutting off your circulation."

"Turtlenecks are classic." I smoothed a hand over my hair, patting it back into place.

"Aunt Francine looked fantastic in them," he said. "They did wonders for her chins." He reached down and tapped me under the chin with the back of his hand. "I can see why you thought Francine was family. There's an uncanny resemblance."

"Yeah, you got her hairline," I said.

Beckett frowned and ran a hand through his wavy locks. He was so vain about his hair; it was hilarious. "Don't worry. Lacey said she loved bald men." I glanced at his stomach. "And beer bellies, too."

He frowned at me. "Too bad you're such a brat. If you would have been nice, I would have let you in the locker room before the fight."

A shiver ran over my skin. "No need. I'm not going to the fight."

Beckett faked a laugh. "Very funny."

"I'm serious. I won't be attending Fight Night."

His brow furrowed, and he pushed his glasses up on his nose to look at me. "The entire town is coming to the fight. It's sold out."

I scrunched up my nose. "Oh? And here I am without a ticket."

Beckett crossed his arms over his chest and glared down at me. "You're really not going?"

"No." I shrugged into my blazer and headed to the door.

"Shit." Beckett clenched his jaw. "He rejected you, didn't he?" Smacking his fist into his palm, he shook his head. "Now I'm going to have to beat his ass."

"I'm touched by your concern, but he didn't reject me." I cleared my throat, feeling it close in on my air. "I'm just not going to the fight."

Beckett's brows drew together over the frames of his glasses. "Why? You're clearly in love with him and have been for half your life."

"That's ..." I stopped talking before a lie could tumble out. "None of your business."

"Maybe not, but you're my sister, and I want you to be happy. Life's too short not to grab onto happiness, especially when it's right next door."

"Ha ha, funny." I reached for the door to my office. "Good neighbor joke."

"Don't do this to him. He needs to see you there."

A cold feeling spread through my chest, and I felt tears threaten. I dropped my hand from the door and turned to face

Beckett. "He said it didn't matter if I came or not. He said it was no big deal."

A bark of laughter escaped his mouth. "That's a load of shit."

"What?"

"He wants you there. Trust me."

Tears came to my eyes. "I can't," I said, swallowing hard and starting again. "I can't watch him get beat up. What if something horrible happens? What if he dies?"

Beckett crossed the room to stand in front of me. He stooped so that we were at eye level. "Jay won't let that happen. I won't let that happen."

"Thatcher has panic attacks," I said, feeling horrible for revealing his secret. "He could have one in the ring."

"I know," Beckett said, surprising me.

"You know?"

"Yeah," he said. "Jay knows, too. We're handling it."

I narrowed my eyes at him. "How?"

"We've been working on some strategies when we spar, techniques that have been proven to work. And he's watched tons of videos with techniques."

A spark of anger flared up. "That's bullshit. No video is gonna help him when he has an attack."

"The techniques are more than he's ever had before."

A heavy weight sat on my chest, making it hard to breathe.

"Thatcher can handle himself. He is not going to get a beatdown. Have you seen the man in the ring?" He whipped out his phone and adjusted his glasses. "Check this out."

Tilting his screen at me, he hit Play on a video of Thatcher and Jay training.

Jay was tall and powerfully built, with mountainous shoulders and thick muscles covered in swirling ink. Thatcher was shorter and cut from a different cloth. His muscled torso was lean and sculpted, chiseled to perfection. Sweat glistened on his skin, and his expression was the picture of fierce concentration.

He prowled the ring, waiting for Jay to strike. Thatcher

looked like a different version of the man I knew. His stance was aggressive yet relaxed, and his eyes were fixed with determination. It sent a shiver down my spine to see him like this. So commanding and powerful yet perfectly at ease and confident.

It was kind of hot.

My breath hitched, and I jabbed the screen to pause the video. "That doesn't prove anything."

Beckett laughed at my reaction. "The women go crazy for him on social media. Did you see his photo shoot?"

"This one had ten thousand likes," Beckett said, showing me a shot of Thatcher in profile, framed by the vineyard backdrop. He had a far-off look in his eyes, conveying a casual confidence. He radiated unworried Zen that matched the scenic background.

Thatcher was that man most of the time. Strong and steady. Calm and quietly commanding. Except I'd seen him when he wasn't. I'd seen him when he was frozen with panic and unable to breathe.

"I'm not saying he's not a good fighter. I'm just worried he'll get caught off guard." Tears swam in front of my eyes as I remembered the stunned look on his face when I'd hit him and the few moments after when he was gone. He'd checked out. And if he did that in a fight, he would be unprotected.

"Don't worry," Beckett said.

"Can't we give a donation?" I asked. "That would fix everything."

"I've already given a donation," Beckett said. "At this point, it's not about the money. It's a whole event. It would look bad for the gym if it got canceled."

"So you care more about the gym than your friend?"

"Peppy."

His use of my old nickname brought a lump to my throat. I blinked back tears and gazed up at my brother. "What?"

"This is Thatcher's decision. He needs to do this for his own reasons. Have faith in him. He can handle this." Beckett reached for the door and pulled it open. "He can win. But if you have any feelings for him at all, you need to be there to support him."

My emotions tangled in a knot as I watched my brother walk away. I couldn't handle seeing Thatcher fight, but what if Beckett was right? What if Thatcher needed me there to win?

Thirty-Six

I stepped onto the scale and held my breath, waiting for the official results. I was at one-seventy-eight that morning, but I'd spent hours on the exercise bike and in the steam room sweating off the pounds. If I didn't make weight, there wouldn't be a fight.

"One-hundred-seventy-four pounds," the official announced.

I let out the breath I'd been holding and stepped off the scale. At fifteen pounds lighter than usual, I felt stronger than ever. I also felt hungry. Very hungry.

"Can I have that pizza now?" I asked Jay.

"After the fight." He gestured at my opponent, who was standing in front of the podium, posing for pictures. "Go get this over with."

Malone and I posed for pictures, glaring at each other.

"I can't wait to mess up that face, Pretty Boy." He sneered. "Let me know if you want to borrow my clippers." Laughing, he flipped a strand of hair near my cheek.

I grimaced and held my ground, refusing to back down under his insults. On paper, he was the clear winner. We were evenly matched in height and weight, but his record was ten and zero with three knockouts, and I hadn't been in the ring in a long time.

The cameras flashed in our faces, and when they were finished, Malone walked away without a word. He didn't even have enough respect for me to trade insults once the eyes were off us.

"Drink up," Jay said, handing me a tall bottle of green juice.

I rolled my eyes. "I wish it was pizza."

"Just pretend."

"No amount of pretending will make this taste like anything but grass."

"Don't argue."

I pinched my nose closed and swallowed as much of the drink as I could manage. My stomach revolted about halfway through, and I handed the bottle back to Jay.

"That's better than nothing," Jay said. "I'll see you back at the gym."

I pulled on my sweatpants and laced up my sneakers. The gym was two miles from the community center where we'd held the weigh-in, and Jay had insisted I jog the distance back to stay loose.

"Take it easy. Don't sprint," he said.

I had no intention of sprinting. I planned to use the time on my jog to the gym as meditation. I needed to clear my mind of everything going on in my life and focus on the fight.

But I couldn't get Pressly out of my head.

I'd told her it wasn't a big deal if she didn't come, but she had to know I was lying. I was the world's worst liar. My face gave me away every time.

At the gym, Jay put me on a stationary bike, insisting I stay loose and keep warm. Shortly after I started on the bike, Beckett arrived with a jelly donut. It wasn't pizza, but it would do. I scarfed it down before Jay could see and spoke around a mouthful to Beckett.

"You think she's gonna come?" I asked.

Beckett knew who I was talking about and didn't try to pretend. "I don't know," he said.

I wasn't surprised. Pressly had already told me she wasn't coming, but I was still hoping she'd change her mind.

"Don't worry about her," Beckett said. "Everyone else will be here. Lacey's on her way right now with the rest of your book club, and everyone from Champion's Corner is here."

I hated to be stuck backstage during the kids' debut fights, but Summer had promised to record them for me so I could watch it later. I'd thought time would drag while I was waiting in the locker room for my fight to start, but before I knew it, they were playing my song. It was time to walk out.

The music filled me with energy, and the cheering crowd silenced the fears in my head. Emotion filled me as I walked down the aisle toward the ring. I felt my father looking down on me, proud of me as he'd always been.

"Pretty Boy!" the crowd shouted as the spotlight shined down on me.

"Watch out for those combos," Beckett said over the cheers. "Remember his left hook."

Beckett and I had analyzed Malone's every strength and weakness. I was as prepared as I could be. But one punch could end me.

Or him.

Anything could happen.

After a quick inspection of my gloves and mouthpiece, the referee motioned me toward my corner of the ring. I ducked under the ropes and shifted from one foot to the other, staying loose as the music changed to Malone's song.

The crowd cheered their approval as he strutted out of his dressing room, raising his gloved hands and gesturing for more.

His fans obliged, screaming his name and stomping their feet hard enough to shake the floor.

Malone worked as a bouncer in a nightclub; I owned a bookstore. He definitely had the sexier profession and more fans, but none of that mattered. Once the fight started, we were just two men in the ring.

"Use your reach to your advantage," Beckett said.

Jay checked my gloves one last time as Malone ducked under the ropes. "Don't let your guard down. I'll be in there to break it up if something happens."

I nodded at Jay; we didn't need to clarify. He meant if I broke down and lost my shit, he would come to my rescue, but of course, he didn't say that.

Malone strutted around the ring, posing and flexing for his fans. Meanwhile, my gaze strayed to the VIP tables set up close to the ring. The kids from the team occupied one table, and the next one was filled with my book club friends. There was Lacey, Gabi, Mia, Kennedy, and Sloane.

My favorite people in the world, all at one table.

Everyone except the one I wanted to see the most.

Thirty-Seven

I settled down with a romantic-comedy movie and a bowl of popcorn, hoping to distract myself from the fact that everyone I knew and loved was at Fight Night.

Within minutes, I'd lost the train of the plot and abandoned my popcorn. Aslan watched me from his bed beside the fireplace, his doggie eyebrow raised in accusation.

"Don't give me that look," I told him, pacing across the room to the kitchen. That was no good because I could see into Thatcher's backyard, and that made me think of him.

My phone rang with Summer's ringtone, and I lunged across the table to grab it.

"Hey," I said, nearly out of breath. "Everything okay?"

"Yeah!" Summer's voice was loud over the noise in the background. "It's great!"

Lately, whenever I heard Summer's ringtone, my entire body clenched in preparation to deal with bad news.

"Are you still at work?" she asked.

"No." I'd told Summer I had to work late and that's why I wasn't going to the fight.

"When are you getting here?"

"Um. I don't think I should come."

"But Dumptruck is gonna fight. And Iceman. You don't want to miss them."

She neglected to mention the main fight, which didn't get by me. "And Thatcher?" I asked. "Have you seen him?"

"Not yet." Her voice quieted, and I could tell she'd moved away from the rest of the crowd. "Um, Mom?"

I stiffened, recognizing that tone of voice. "What is it?"

"I think you should get here before Mr. T's fight."

"Oh?" My throat felt like it was closing up. "Why's that?"

"Because he wants you here."

I shook my head. "He said it didn't matter if I came or not."

"But he loves you," she blurted.

My mouth fell open. "What? Did he tell you that?"

"No." She was quiet for a moment. "I did something bad."

I'd been pacing the kitchen, but I stopped as panic gripped my chest. "What did you do?"

Summer sniffed, and I could tell she was crying. "I was borrowing dog food from Thatcher because you forgot to buy it again, and I found an envelope with your name on it, and I took it." Her words came out in a jumbled rush, each one tripping over the other. "And it was full of letters, and I read them, and I hid them."

A wave of dizziness crashed over me. "Thatcher's letters?"

"I'm really sorry," she said. "They weren't mine, and I know I shouldn't have read them."

"Where are the letters now?" I asked, already tearing up the stairs to her room.

"I hid them," she said.

I threw open her door and looked into her room. It was so tidy I didn't see where she could hide anything. Her bookshelf was arranged by color, and her bed was neatly made.

Dropping to my knees, I looked under her bed. There was nothing there.

"Summer?" I asked, sitting back on my haunches. "Where did you hide the letters?"

"In the treehouse." She sniffed again. "I'm sorry."

"It's okay," I said, flying down the stairs and out the back door.

"Are you coming?" she asked.

"I don't know."

My heart felt like it was being torn into pieces. Maybe Thatcher did want me there and he was just trying to play it cool when he said it was no big deal.

But I still wasn't sure if I could watch the man I loved in a fight.

"Are you gonna marry him? Like Dad and Jennifer?"

I paused at the bottom of the tree house. Marriage was something I never thought I would do more than once, but Thatcher might make me reconsider. Of course, we'd never discussed it, so I was probably jumping the gun. But he was the only man I could picture sharing my life with.

"Would that be okay with you if I did?"

There was a long pause. "Yes," she said finally. "I think that would be okay. Maybe Aslan and Daisy can be in the wedding."

I hung my head, laughing a little. "Let's not get carried away. I don't know what's gonna happen."

"Just get here," Summer said, wise beyond her years. "And hurry."

I hung up and climbed into the tree house. Inside, Summer had laid out a blanket and pillow next to a cardboard box of books. There was a suspicious lump under the blanket, and I lifted it to find the large envelope with my name on it.

Sure enough, it was open. When I turned it upside down, six letters spilled out.

They were addressed to Peppy Vinroot care of Pete Hayes. I examined the handwriting, picturing the young man writing my name, entrusting his deepest thoughts to me.

I slipped the first one out and read it quickly, smiling a little at the formal signature.

Sincerely, Thatcher Hayes.

I devoured the next letter and then the next, reading them in order of the postmarks. Tears slipped down my cheeks as I read his words. He'd been so young. So brave.

There was a Polaroid picture just like the one I'd seen at Alika's. Thatcher, with his shorn head and lips pressed together in a serious, grown-up expression, flanked by his two friends.

He'd laid his heart on his sleeve for me, and I'd never even known it.

Anger and frustration mounted at Pete Hayes, who'd kept these letters from me. But it was pointless being mad at a dead man. I couldn't go back in time and change anything that had happened.

And wouldn't if I could. Because... Summer. She wouldn't exist if I'd seen these letters years ago.

I read the last letter, my heart nearly bursting with emotion as I read the last line.

My belly tightened, and my head ached. I didn't think I could stomach watching the fight, but I knew I had no choice.

He needed me.

Moving with more speed than I thought I possessed, I raced into the house and grabbed my purse. My leggings and oversized sweater weren't ideal, but I didn't want to waste time changing.

"Hang tight, Aslan," I said, rushing back to check his water bowl. "I'll be back soon."

In the garage, I shoved my feet into a pair of boots and hit the button for the garage door. Too impatient to wait for it to open, I squeezed around the front of my car and slid behind the wheel.

Once seated, I took a moment to breathe. There was no use driving like a maniac. It wouldn't help anyone if I got in a wreck on my way to the fight. Safety first.

I started the car and glanced in the rearview mirror. The garage door was still closed, so I hit the button in my car and shifted into reverse.

The garage door was taking forever to open, and then I realized it wasn't opening. Something was wrong. I groaned in frustration. My dream house was trying to sabotage me.

And then I spotted my bike against the side door. I hadn't ridden it in so long; I wasn't sure I remembered how.

But I had to try.

July 2002

Dear Peppy,

This is going to be my last letter for a while. I don't know what's happening, or even who I am anymore these days.

I made a friend with one of the boys we rescued. We read books together. He liked Shakespeare, Tupac Shakur, and limericks.

His name was Josiah.

But he wasn't my friend. He waited until my guard was down to steal my weapon. He went on a rampage, killing almost everyone at the rehabilitation school.

I was just beginning to think these kids could be saved. But now I know—they aren't children, they are monsters.

Part of me wishes I would have died with the rest of my unit, but then I would never see you again.

Everything was my fault. People are dead because of me.

I'm not sure I can live with this, but I know I don't want to live without you. Your kindness and nurturing heart might be the only thing that can save me.

If you ever cared for me at all (and I haven't totally scared you off with these letters), come find me.

I need you.

Sincerely, Thatcher Hayes

The bell to end the first round rang, and I stalked back to my corner. At the start of the fight, I felt invincible, but as I sank onto the stool in my corner, the adrenaline rush faded and pain set in. Malone had landed too many punches. He'd won that round, and now I had to come from behind.

The thought made my breath shallow and darkness threaten to take over, but I closed my eyes and pictured myself in a happy place. My bookstore, the lake, my bed with Pressly in my arms.

I opened my eyes and blinked slowly. I was okay.

"Watch the left hook," Beckett said.

I nodded. The left hook was going to destroy me if he connected.

Malone's hits packed a punch. He was just as strong as he looked and quicker on his feet than I'd anticipated.

I spit out my mouthpiece and guzzled down the water Jay poured into my mouth.

"He's killing me," I said.

"You're still in this," Jay said, inspecting a cut on my cheek. "Stop walking into his fists, and everything will be fine."

My heart pounded furiously.

"You solid?" Jay took my chin and forced my gaze up to his.

I pushed away the panic at the fringes of my mind and looked him dead in the eye. "I'm good."

"Take him out, Pretty Boy." Jay grinned. He loved grinding on me about my nickname. "One lucky punch," he said. "Lay the fucker out."

"There's no such thing as luck," I said, gesturing at Beckett for my mouthpiece. I was done talking. It was time to fight.

Malone opened up the second round with a lunging assault aimed at my torso, but he wasn't quick enough to land anything. I danced out of his way and took my shot—a quick right hook to his exposed cheek.

It only stunned him. If I wanted to win, I'd have to do better than that.

He laughed off my punch and dropped his arms to his sides, taunting me. "Is that all you got?"

I stepped closer and delivered a combo to his face and body before he could get his hands up. Blood poured from his nose, and he laughed even harder, implying he'd given me those punches out of sympathy. I ignored his antics and swung at him again, putting everything I had into the punch.

He ducked and slammed his fists into my ribs, taking my breath away.

I staggered back, and he pressed forward.

"Watch the left hook," Beckett yelled from my corner.

Adrenaline surged through me, and I ducked just as Malone's left fist hooked toward my temple.

"Move your feet," Beckett yelled.

My feet moved, and I sidestepped another punch just in time.

We traded punches for the next thirty seconds that felt like forever. The crowd exploded with cheers every time one of us landed a blow. Blood ran into my eyes from a cut on my forehead. My ribs screamed in agony every time I twisted to throw a punch.

"Get him, Mr. T!"

Warmth spread through my chest at the sound of Summer's voice raised above the others. I took my eyes off Malone for a split second and looked in the direction of her table where she sat with the other kids from Champion's Corner.

The confidence in her smile made me feel invincible. But it was the woman standing behind her that made my world tilt.

Pressly.

She stood just behind the VIP table, looking adorably disheveled, carrying a pizza box.

She raised her arm to wave, a tentative smile breaking out over her face.

"Watch the hook!"

Beckett's warning registered a moment before Malone's fist slammed into my head. Pain rocketed through me, and then the ground rose up to meet my face. I threw my hands out just in time to catch my fall. My hands and knees took the brunt of my weight, and breath exploded from my lungs.

"One!" the referee's first count sounded. "Two!"

"Get up!" Beckett yelled.

"Stay down!" Malone screamed, strutting around the canvas, pretending to shave his head.

Pressly's face swam before my eyes. She was saying something, but it was impossible to hear over the crowd. At first, I thought she was saying stay down, siding with Malone out of fear, but then I realized it was the opposite. She was screaming for me to fight, and she was so agitated she nearly dropped the pizza box.

I struggled to my feet, wobbling a little before finding my balance. Malone danced behind the referee, taunting me.

The referee asked if I could fight, and I met his gaze with fierce determination.

"Fight," the referee said.

Malone beckoned me forward. "Shoulda stayed down, Pretty Boy!" He raised his arms, asking the crowd to cheer, and it was exactly the opening I needed for a lucky punch.

Rearing back, I drove a right cross straight into his chin. I felt the connection ricochet up my arm to my shoulder, and pain erupted down my right side.

His eyes rolled back in his head, and he tipped backward, landing hard enough on the mat to make it shake beneath my feet.

The next few seconds were a blur as the referee counted and Malone didn't stir. "Ten!"

The medics rushed the mat as Malone finally sat up, shaking his head. I stared at him, not quite believing I'd won.

And then with a lightning crack of emotion, I realized I'd done it. I'd faced down Malone and my fears, and I was the champion.

The fans were on their feet, screaming, but only one voice mattered. I searched the crowd and located Pressly, jumping up and down with the rest of the kids from the team.

The celebration rang in my ears as Beckett and Jay swarmed me and raised my arms in the air. I winced as my injured ribs sang in protest. But the pain was drowned out by the sense of satisfaction filling my entire body.

It was one of the best moments of my life. Unforgettable.

I found Pressly in the crowd, and we exchanged a long look. The MC was waiting to announce my victory, and Malone had finally struggled to his feet. It would have been the right thing to do to shake his hand and accept my victory, but fuck doing the right thing.

I strode across the mat and ducked under the ropes, pushing through the crowd of fans to get to Pressly. A huge smile lit her face, and she practically launched herself into my arms. I caught her and crushed my mouth to hers, feeling on top of the world.

The kiss was not exactly suitable for public, but I didn't care about the scene we were making. I only cared about Pressly.

I groaned as fresh pain flared up in my injured mouth.

"Sorry," she said, her hands fluttering over my face, pausing on the bruises. "Are you okay?"

"I'm fine." I smiled through the pain. "I'm great."

"Hey, Pretty Boy!" Jay called from the ring. "You gonna come up here and claim your prize?"

I tightened my arms around Pressly. As far as I was concerned, I already had.

Thatcher sat on top of a table in a relaxed pose, hands resting on his knees, head and shoulders leaning against the wall. His damp hair was slicked back from his face, and he wore an unzipped sweatshirt and gray sweatpants. Both his eyes were bruised, and white bandages circled his ribs.

"Is that still hot?" he asked, eyeing the pizza box I carried.

"I doubt it." I put the box on the table and moved to stand between his legs. "You don't know what I had to do to get this."

He cocked one eyebrow and fitted his hands to my waist possessively. "Yeah?"

"I robbed a teenager for this and pretended I was the delivery person to get in without a ticket."

He laughed and then stopped abruptly, clutching his ribs.

"How bad does it hurt?" I grazed my knuckles over the bandages, wanting to kiss every inch of his bruised skin.

"Ever had a broken rib?" he asked on a sigh, catching my fingers.

"No."

He kissed my knuckles. "It hurts pretty fucking bad."

I spread my hand over his cheek, fingers feather light on his raw, angry skin. "I was in labor for twenty-one hours," I said. "Not much can top that."

He chuckled dryly, wincing. Then his eyes found mine, his gaze like warm honey over my skin.

"I'm glad you showed up," he said, scooting off the table to gather me to his chest.

"I didn't want to," I said. "But Summer convinced me."

He pulled back and looked at me. "Did she?" He smiled. "How?"

I smoothed his damp hair back from his face. "She read your letters," I said.

His entire body tensed. "Shit."

I framed his face in my hands and tilted it down to mine. "It's okay."

He dropped his head. "She must have seen the envelope with your name on it."

"She took them and then hid them in the tree house."

The color drained from his face, making his bruises stand out in stark relief against his pale skin. "You read them?"

I nodded. "I had to read fast because I didn't want to miss your fight, and then my garage door wouldn't open, and I had to ride my bike, and—" I paused to breathe, aware that this was one of those moments that would change my life forever and I was rambling on like an idiot. "And so, here I am. With pizza," I finished lamely.

His eyes locked on mine, staring as he tried to process everything I'd just said.

"You read them?" he asked again, bracing himself for my answer.

Sadness for the boy he'd been thrummed like a string across my heart. "I read every word."

He glanced away, looking at the wall behind my head, then the floor, then the wall again. His shoulders began to shake, and I realized he was crying, holding back sobs. "And you still came?" he asked, his tear-filled eyes finding mine. "Even after what I did?"

My heart broke in two, and a sob tore through my chest. "You were just a kid, Thatcher." I pulled him into my arms, wrapping him tightly in my embrace. "It wasn't your fault."

He buried his head against my shoulder, his entire body shaking with silent sobs. I stroked my hands up his back, threaded my fingers through his hair, held him close. Tears streamed down my cheeks as I cried for that boy soldier who'd seen such tragedy and that pretty girl who'd waited on her dad's boat for hours in the freezing cold.

I eased back, smoothing my hands over his cheeks to dry his tears. "I'm sorry."

He shook his head. "Why?"

"Because I missed the whole first half of the fight."

He cracked a smile. "You didn't miss much," he said. "I was getting my ass beat." His smile bloomed a little, overshadowing the tears. "You came," he said. "That's all that matters."

I wiped away the last of his tears. "Because you needed me."

His eyes widened, and then he kissed me so hard it took my breath away. It seemed we couldn't stop kissing. Or touching. Our lips came together in a brutal crush, our hands feverishly sliding over each other.

He yanked my sweater up, filling his hands with my breasts. I slid my leg up and over his hip, shamelessly climbing him.

The door opened, and Jay interrupted us, clearing his throat. "Yo, man," he said. "Cassandra needs you to come out for your interview."

Thatcher sighed. "Give me ten minutes."

Jay headed to the door. "You've got five," he said, pulling the door closed behind him.

I framed Thatcher's face in my hands. "Five minutes isn't going to be nearly long enough."

His eyes shined down at me, open and bright. "Good thing we have forever."

Epilogue

Two months later

A sharp bark awakened me. I opened my eyes and saw Aslan standing on my pillow, his tongue mere inches from my face. His hot doggy breath bathed my cheeks.

"Mom! Wake up!" Summer bounced onto the bed.

"I'm up." I pushed my hair off my face and glanced at the clock. "What's going on? Are we late for school?"

"No, silly!" Summer bounced on the bed again. "It's Saturday."

"Oh." I sank back under the covers, eager to snatch a few more minutes of sleep.

Summer was having none of it. She jumped off the bed and threw my covers back. I hadn't seen her this excited since Christmas morning a few years ago.

She tugged my hand and pulled me from the bed. "Come on! You have to see."

I shoved my feet into slippers and grabbed my robe. "What's so important?" I asked as she dragged me down the hall.

Aslan hurried behind us, nudging my calves with his nose to speed us up. We raced down the steps and to the front door.

"Close your eyes," Summer said as she put her hand on the door.

I closed my eyes and took her hand, allowing her to lead me outside. June had blown in with warm days and cool mornings. The nip in the air had me pulling my robe tight around my middle. Summer told me to step down three steps, and then we were on the grassy lawn. "Where are you taking me?" I asked, hoping none of our nosy neighbors were peeking out their window at the crazy single mom in the yard in her robe and slippers.

"Almost there," she said.

I felt the roots of the giant oak under my feet and heard the quiet rustle of the leaves in the breeze. Aslan barked, and the sharp sound of Daisy's bark answered. A smile stole over my lips because where there was Daisy, there was Thatcher.

I struggled to keep my eyes closed as Summer squeezed my hand and tugged me a few more steps. "Stop," she said. "Open your eyes."

I blinked my eyes open, and the first thing I saw was Thatcher, standing under the tall limbs of the mighty oak, wearing a backwards baseball hat and a sly grin. He raised his chin at me, his eyes gleaming brightly. "What do you think?"

It was then that I noticed the chain he leaned on, which was connected on one end to a branch high in the tree and on the other to a shiny black tire.

My hand flew to my mouth, and I glanced down at Summer. She let out a whoop of delight and ran to the swing, giving it a tug. "Do you like it?"

I nodded. The tears clogging my throat made it impossible to speak.

"Want to try it out?" Summer asked.

A shiver of pleasure sliced through me at the sight of my daughter standing at the tire swing. The dogs ran in the yard behind her, chasing a squirrel and barking happily. A slight breeze made my robe flutter, but it was my heart that was doing the dance. Because the man of my dreams stood in front of the tree, smiling at me.

"You go first," I told Summer, wanting to bask in the glow of my dreams coming true.

Things hadn't gone according to plan, and I'd hit a few bumps along the way. My dream house had turned out to be a lemon, and the father of my child a useless human, but Summer and I were closer than ever, and my neighbor was the hottest man in Mossy Oak.

"No, Mom," Summer said, hopping off the swing. "I want you to go first."

Thatcher reached up to grab the chain and held it steady, nodding for me to climb on. I tucked my robe tighter around me and walked over to the swing.

Grabbing the chain with both hands, I climbed on and hung my legs over the side. I'd always wondered what it felt like to sit in the tire swing. How many times had I driven past this house and envied the girl who swung under the branches of the mighty oak, oblivious to the world's problems?

How many times had I imagined she was me?

"You ready?" Thatcher's voice sounded in my ear.

I turned my face to his, and he dropped a kiss onto my lips. Summer giggled in the background, and the sound made a giddy thrill rush through me. "I'm ready."

He gave me a gentle push that sent me swinging. I leaned back in and smelled the new rubber scent of the tire and freshly cut grass. Patchy spots of blue showed through the budding green leaves of the oak tree. Summer's laugh sounded, followed by Aslan's happy bark.

It was the moment I'd always dreamed of. I was flying high. If I fell, Thatcher's strong arms were ready to catch me.

WANT TO READ MORE OF THATCHER AND PRESSLY?

Sign up for Jill's newsletter and get this Bonus Scene told from Thatcher's point of view.

About the Author

Jill Brashear is a hopeless romantic and author of swoon-worthy contemporary romances that will leave you breathless. With a pen in her hand and a heart full of love, Jill weaves tales of passion, longing, and happily-ever-afters that will make your heart skip a beat.

Also by Jill Brashear

ALOHA SERIES

Try Easy

Try Me

Try Right

Try Over

BLUE RIDGE BOOK CLUB SERIES

Love, Lacey Donovan

XOXO, Valentina

Blue Collar Crush

STANDALONES

Win, Lose, or Love

Jock Seeks Geek